Rescue was on the way!

Miles fiddled with the binoculars to get a better focus. It was a long, sleek boat that rode low in the water. There seemed to be three people in the boat. Was that his father standing at the helm, and his mother, her hair blowing in the breeze? He couldn't believe it. Was it a mirage? He looked again. It was real! Rescue was on the way!

Collect *ESCAPE FROM LOST ISLAND*
Available from HarperPaperbacks

Escape!

Clay Coleman

HarperPaperbacks

A Division of HarperCollins*Publishers*

This is a work of fiction. The characters, incidents, and dialogues are products of the author's imagination and are not to be construed as real. Any resemblance to actual events or persons, living or dead, is entirely coincidental.

HarperPaperbacks *A Division of* HarperCollins*Publishers*
                 10 East 53rd Street, New York, N.Y. 10022

Produced by Daniel Weiss Associates, Inc.
33 West 17th Street, New York, New York 10011.

RL 4.8   IL 008–012
First printing: April, 1991

Printed in the United States of America

HarperPaperbacks and colophon are trademarks of
HarperCollins*Publishers*

10 9 8 7 6 5 4 3 2 1

One

Miles Bookman had been up all night, standing guard. The blond-haired boy of fourteen was watching the southern horizon. Deep trouble lay to the south—on Lost Island.

A gentle, tropical wind pushed in from the water. The sun was rising to the east. Miles watched the sea birds that rode the currents of balmy air against the orange sky. He wished he could fly away from the island as easily as they could.

Miles sighed and sat down in the sand. His whole body ached from exhaustion, but he couldn't close his eyes and go to sleep. He had to keep watching until Len Hayden came down from the compound to relieve him as sentry.

As the morning light grew brighter, Miles took out a worn notebook and began to write with a stubby pencil.

"Journal of Miles Bookman. I'd write down the date, but I don't know it. It could be Saturday or Sunday. Who knows? Since we were marooned on this island, time doesn't mean much. All that matters is that we have been fighting for our lives, and so far we have been lucky. I'm only writing this down in case somebody finds us dead."

Miles paused for a moment, trying to sort it all out. The images swirled in his head. Sometimes it all seemed like a dream. But then the roar of the waves would mock him, reminding Miles that his predicament was all too real.

"It all began when we left Fiji. My father hired a plane to take us back to Hawaii. Len and I had been on summer vacation from Dover Academy in Portsmouth, New Hampshire. The plane stopped in Majoru, in the Marshall Islands. We picked up some other kids, juvenile delinquents who had been in a work camp. . . ."

Taking a deep breath, Miles recalled the dark impressions of the plane crash. The old C-47 had flown straight into a storm. He could see the water below the belly of the aircraft, getting closer and closer.

"I swam ashore after the crash. I found Len on another part of Lost Island. . . . Then we met up with Meat Hook and the bandits.

"We couldn't believe it at first. Meat Hook and his men are monsters. We didn't understand how they got here until Kirkland and the others freed us from the hanging bamboo cages.

"When we escaped, we stole a boat and sailed

2

north to the place known as Apocalypse Island, where I am writing this now. We discovered the compound that sits on the plateau above the beach. I found computer records in the lab building. I figured out that some scientists did experiments here. They were trying to develop a serum that would turn criminals into good people. Only the serum made them worse. The criminals revolted against the scientists. Now they live on Lost Island to the south."

A shiver played across Miles's shoulders, making him stop for a moment. He peered to the south, wondering how long it would take for Meat Hook and his men to return. He lowered his head again and went back to his work.

"Meat Hook is like something out of a horror movie. He has a long scar down his face. An American eagle has been tattooed on his chest. He carries an iron hook in his right hand. Bullet Head is his sidekick. He's fat and wears a steel helmet. I've never known real fear in my life—until I saw these men and their followers. One of the scientists, a man named Cyrus Albright, came back to try to help them. He had another serum. The serum cured me when I was shot with an arrow by one of the mutants. They killed Dr. Albright and destroyed his ship, a high-tech vessel called the *Proteus*. Proteus was also the name of the project conducted by the scientists. It's the name of an ancient, mythical god who could transform into different shapes."

Miles lifted his hand from the page. He flexed his fingers to drive the cramps away. He had to keep writing. Somehow it made him feel better to put it all down.

"Nine of us survived the crash. Joey Wolfe, Cruiser, D. J., Pee Wee, and Digger are dead. Vinnie might as well be dead. He was captured by the bandits. Vinnie decided to join the mutants and become one of them. He calls himself Razorback now. I'm not sure about Kirkland. His fate is still unknown to me. He was captured by Meat Hook during the last raid. Len and I hid in our underground pits, but Kirkland was afraid so he took his chances in the jungle. Augie said the mutants got Kirkland—he might be dead or alive.

"Augie is another story. He's the youngest survivor, only twelve. We thought he was dead when he fell off the mountain. But he lived and he found a wild dog he named Commando. They became friends. When Commando killed the leader of another dog pack, the dogs began to follow Augie. He lives with them in the jungle. They have saved our skins more than once, but they are unpredictable. Sometimes they disappear for days."

A chattering sound drew Miles from the page. He glanced over his shoulder. A dense jungle rose behind the beach. Birds and monkeys were coming to life in the early morning air. The scientists had left behind wildlife and fruit trees that helped the boys to survive. There were also supplies in a secret chamber in the basement of the lab.

"We've been able to stay alive," Miles continued. "We hoped for rescue and it finally came. My father hired a pilot named Branch Colgan to find us. Only his plane crashed in the desert. Len and I found him and took him to the lab. I used the last of Professor Albright's serum to heal him. He fought with Kirkland and became the leader. We all went back to the other end of the island where the hangar is located. Using the secret password, Proteus, I managed to open the hangar. It's a large, space-age dome, and there was a plane inside. We took the plane to the desert and got it flying. For a little while, it looked like we were going to get off this island. But then Razorback came out of nowhere. He threw a rock that hit Colgan in the head. Colgan has amnesia now. Kirkland and Cruiser stole the plane, but they didn't know Razorback had stowed away. He made the plane crash. Cruiser was killed—eaten by a shark, Kirkland said. Razorback escaped. We went after Kirkland and captured him with Augie's help. He was found guilty of betraying us. We put him on a raft and sent him out to sea. Kirkland went back to Lost Island. He saw that Vinnie had been put in a cage. Kirkland freed him, but when they tried to escape, Vinnie fought him. Vinnie's a mutant now. Kirkland somehow got back here with his

5

life. But now he's been captured, like I said. I don't know what happened to him. I'm not sure I want to know."

Miles took a moment to read what he had written. He had left out some of the details. There was so much to remember and every memory was painful.

"Colgan, the pilot, has disappeared again. He imagines that he sees this girl named Mae. I'm sure it's because he was whacked on the head with that rock. I hope he'll come out of his trance—if we ever see him again.

"If we ever see *anyone* again it will be a miracle. According to Colgan, the army doesn't want anyone coming out into this section of the Pacific. These islands are off the main shipping lanes. We haven't seen one sign of a ship or a plane, except for Colgan's crash. I know my father will keep trying to find us. He's a famous photojournalist, so I know he has contacts all over the world. But even he might be limited if no one will help him.

"Who will come for us? Who will rescue us from this nightmare? I hate this island. I don't even know how we've made it this long. Meat Hook will surely return to kill us. We can't keep hiding forever. If I am dead and someone is reading this, go to Lost Island, eliminate Meat Hook and the bandits. Avenge my death. Wipe the mutants off the face of the earth. Make sure they never kill anyone again. Tell my father and mother that I love them. I am writing this with a sane mind. I only hope I stay that way. God help us if we are going to survive."

Miles signed the entry in his journal and then closed the notebook. His eyes lifted again to the south. For a moment, he thought he saw a sail against the orange sky. But it was only the wing span of a large sea bird.

Miles was about to stand up when he heard squeaking footsteps in the sand. He glanced back over his shoulder to see Len Hayden coming toward him. Len was a tall boy of fifteen. He wore a glum expression on his tanned face.

Len sat down beside Miles, focusing his blue eyes on the horizon. "Any noise from mutant land?"

Miles shook his head. "Negative."

Len sighed. "I thought you were going to watch from the top of the lab building."

"I did for a while," Miles replied. "I just felt like being down here when the sun came up."

Len nodded. "I can take over now."

"Where's Augie?" Miles asked.

Len shrugged. "Who knows? He was there with his dogs last night, but when I woke up, he was gone again. He just keeps getting stranger and stranger, Bookman. I don't know about him."

"Augie hasn't hurt anyone," Miles replied. "Unless you count the mutants."

Len shuddered. Commando and the dog pack

had put more than one bandit in a shallow grave. But there was no guarantee that the dogs wouldn't turn on Len and Miles some day.

"What about Colgan?" Miles asked. "Any sign of him?"

"No," Len replied. "He hasn't shown up yet. Maybe we should go look for him. He could've gone back to the hangar."

"Maybe later," Miles said.

"What are we going to do, Bookman?"

Miles gazed toward the south. "I don't know. I was thinking about some way to rescue Kirkland. If he's still alive."

Len's eyes grew wide. "Have you lost it? We can't rescue Kirkland. And even if we could, why would we want to try? Kirkland caused a lot of trouble for us. We would have escaped in that plane we found at the hangar if Kirkland hadn't crashed it."

"I know, I know," Miles replied. "But Kirkland was coming around before he got captured. He wanted to help us."

"Too little, too late," Len said. "It's every man for himself, Bookman. You said it yourself."

Miles knew Len was right. They could barely help themselves, much less launch a rescue attempt on Lost Island. They didn't have a boat. There was no way for them to get to the south, even if Kirkland was still alive.

But Miles didn't want to give up hope. He had been the resourceful one. But he seemed to be running out of options. For the first time since they had been marooned on the island, Miles didn't have a plan.

"Why did we ever have to come to Fiji?" Len cried. "Why did we have to get on that plane?"

Miles glared at him. "Are you saying this is all my fault?"

Len turned away. "Who else? I never would have been on that plane if you hadn't taken me on vacation with you."

Miles jumped to his feet. "That's a low blow, Hayden! I asked you to come along to pay you back for all the times I stayed at your house during holidays from school!"

"Yeah, because your actress mother and your big-shot father don't care enough about you to visit during Christmas!"

"Drop dead!" Miles cried.

"Same to you!"

"I don't have to take this!"

"Then get lost!" Len cried.

Miles stomped across the beach, toward the path that led into the jungle. He entered the dense undergrowth, fighting the vines that hung over the trail. His face was still reddened as he passed the grove of fruit trees.

How could Len say that it was all his fault?

He stopped for a moment, gazing down at one of the mantraps that they had built to trap the mutants. Miles could hear the howls of pain

9

and agony in his head. He moved past the traps, heading for the path that rose to the compound.

As he climbed the path, the clear stream bubbled to his left. The water ran down from the mountains. They had been drinking from the stream and using the water to cook.

When he climbed over the edge of the plateau, Miles looked toward the purple peaks of the mountains behind the white lab building. The compound was surrounded on all sides by steep slopes and thick jungle. They were trapped on the plateau.

Tears began to roll down Miles's cheeks. Maybe he'd never see his home and parents again.

Miles turned quickly, peering toward the calm ocean. He wiped his eyes, wondering when the end would really come.

Two

Lieutenant Branch Colgan, United States Coast Guard, lifted his aching head from the sand. His eyes turned quickly to the bright, morning sky as he sat up and stretched.

Colgan didn't know where he was. He glanced up and down the lonely stretch of beach. He couldn't remember how he had gotten there.

Colgan touched the back of his throbbing skull. He felt the wound, the dried blood. Someone had hurt him, but it wasn't clear what had happened. He couldn't recall the boy named Razorback hitting him with a rock.

The waves lapped gently against the white sand. Colgan gazed to the west, across the expanse of the ocean. Images swirled in his head. He half-remembered a large plane soaring through the sky. He saw Len and Miles and Kirkland, their faces alive in his dulled thoughts.

"What happened?" he muttered to himself. "Where am I?"

Staggering toward the surf, Colgan waded into the water. He dunked his head in the cool tidal flow. The salty liquid stung the wound on the back of his skull, but the coolness eased the pain a little.

Colgan looked down at his body. He was wearing khakis and a T-shirt. He looked down and saw the insignia and words printed over his heart.

"Coast Guard," he said aloud.

His eyes narrowed as he tried to remember. Had he been in Hawaii? He remembered the name of Senator Williams. He saw the blue water beneath him and the stranded boat. Had he really been there?

As he started to turn away from the surf, Colgan saw something resting on the beach. It was a long, narrow outrigger canoe. His eyes grew wider. He suddenly remembered how the canoe had gotten there.

"Mae!"

The girl had been with him the day before. They had talked for a long time. She had told him how she had come from Papua, an island to the west. Her canoe had blown away from the island in a storm. She had ended up on this beach with Colgan.

He wheeled around, staring at the rocks behind the sand. The cliffs rose above the beach.

He had climbed over the cliffs to get to the water, to look for Mae.

"Mae?"

Where was she? Maybe the bandits had gotten her. Colgan remembered the evil mutants who had set on them before.

"Mae, are you here?" he shouted.

There was no reply except the sound of the surf. Colgan broke into a run, making for the rocks. He began to search through the large boulders until he saw a flash of the red dress.

"Mae!"

He looked down at the sleeping girl. She had long, thick, black hair, olive skin, dark eyes, and beautiful features. Colgan frowned at her. He had told the other boys that Mae was his girlfriend.

Mae Kahana opened her eyes and looked up at Colgan. Quickly she jumped to her feet.

Colgan smiled at her. "Hi, Mae. Don't be afraid."

"Branch," she replied. "Have we been here all night?"

"We were talking," he told her. "It got dark. You came back here to sleep and I slept on the beach. It's morning now."

Mae nodded her head. "We're lost."

Colgan had another burst of memory. He had come to the island to rescue the boys. An Englishman had hired him to fly the plane. He had crashed in the flat desert.

"Are you all right?" Mae asked.

Colgan put a hand on his forehead. "I don't know. My head is so foggy. Do you want to go home?"

Mae nodded. She had told him that she was fourteen years old. She had never been away from home in her life. "I don't know if I can make it back in that canoe. I'm not even sure which direction to go."

"You said your island was west of here," Colgan replied.

"Yes, but I've never traveled this far."

Colgan exhaled, feeling helpless. Suddenly he remembered that he was twenty-five years old and a graduate of the Coast Guard Academy. He had bucked his superiors to go in search of the missing boys. He had probably ruined his career in the process.

"Branch, are you all right?"

He grimaced. "I keep remembering. It's coming back to me slowly."

"You spoke of the other boys," Mae said. "Are they near here?"

Colgan had to think about it for a moment. "There's a lab," he said finally. "On the other end of the island. I think they're at the lab."

"Maybe we should go there," Mae replied.

Colgan nodded. "Yes. There's food and water. And danger. We have to be careful."

Mae frowned. "My people tell stories of de-

14

mons on these islands. They warn against coming here."

"There are demons all right," Colgan replied. "The scientists created them."

"Let's go," Mae said. "We'll take the canoe to the others. There are two paddles."

Colgan nodded. "Sure. We can make it. I hope the others are still there. I hope the bandits didn't come and get them."

Mae eyed him cautiously. "You saw these bandits?"

Colgan remembered images of desperate, evil men who were dressed in strange costumes. With the other boys, he had killed some of the bandits and buried them in the jungle. There had also been a plane, but something had happened to keep them from flying off the island.

"The plane," he muttered. "Maybe—"

"What plane?" Mae asked.

Colgan shook his head. "Come on, let's get to the southern end of the island. Len and Miles will know what happened."

"Len and Miles," Mae repeated. "I want to meet them. I hope they haven't gone."

"No," Colgan replied. "They're still there. I'm sure of it."

They came away from the rocks and walked to the canoe. Together they launched the vessel into the surf. Colgan got in the back with the broad paddle. Mae sat in the front, dipping her paddle into the water.

They moved out of the shallows into the deeper water beyond the shorebreak. Colgan kept peering to the south. He remembered the other boys talking about the lair of the bandits. What had they called it? Lost Island.

Colgan shuddered. Lost Island. It was not a place he wanted to visit. They kept the canoe moving steadily around the coastline to the other end of the island, where Len and Miles waited at the lab compound.

The soft, morning breezes wafted over the hidden lagoon where the bandits were camped on the beach. The winds rustled the palm-thatch roofs of the huts that served as shelter for Meat Hook and his men. The warm air also stirred through the hanging bamboo cage that held Neil Kirkland prisoner.

Neil Kirkland had been part of the delinquent rehabilitation project that brought him to the Marshall Islands. He had been unlucky enough to board the plane that wrecked off the shore of Lost Island. After several clashes with Meat Hook and his men, Kirkland had finally ended up as a prisoner in the bandit camp.

His hands gripped the bamboo bars of the hanging cell. He hated being locked up like a zoo animal. He had to fight to keep from losing his mind.

Kirkland peered out toward the grass and palm huts that were strewn all over the beach of the hidden lagoon. Beyond the blue water lay the wall of rock. A narrow opening through the rock wall led to the ocean. Behind the clearing and all along the beach was a thick jungle of palm trees and tropical vines. There didn't seem to be any way for Kirkland to escape.

Sweat poured down Kirkland's rugged face. What were the bandits going to do with him? He was terrified. Meat Hook was the kind of sick monster who would string out his torture.

Kirkland lifted his eyes to the boats that were beached at the far end of the bandit camp. Kirkland thought about ways of escaping from the cage. If he could somehow loosen the bamboo bars, he could drop to the ground and steal one of the boats.

His gaze focused on the ropes that had been used to tie the bars together. Using his fingernails, Kirkland began to pick at the ropes. If he could just cut through one of the bindings, he could wedge the bars apart and climb through to freedom. He had to escape. He didn't want to die miserably in the mutant camp.

"Forget it, Kirkland!"

The voice had come from below him. Kirkland looked down to see Vinnie standing on the beach. Vinnie held a crossbow in his hands. He was standing guard over Kirkland.

"Vinnie, let me out of here. We can escape together."

"Razorback!" the red-haired boy replied.

"That's my name now. Vinnie's dead. Razor-back lives."

Kirkland shook his head. "Vinnie, you can't stay with these creeps. They'll kill you!"

Razorback laughed. "These are my brothers!"

"Right," Kirkland scoffed. "When I found you, they had you locked up in this cage!"

"That was a misunderstanding," Razorback said. "But you fixed it, Kirkland. When they found out I wouldn't leave with you—when you thought you were rescuing me—they took me back. Now I'm one of them—forever!"

Kirkland glared at Vinnie. They had been part of the same delinquent program in the Marshall Islands. Vinnie had always been bad, but Kirkland had never imagined that Vinnie was evil to the core.

"You've got a choice," Razorback said. "You can join us, Kirkland. Become one of the broth-erhood."

Kirkland sighed, leaning back against the bars. "You're crazy, Vinnie."

"Razorback! That's my name now. You can have a cool name like me. How about it? Something like—I don't know—how about Franken-stein?"

"Drop dead, Vinnie!"

Razorback pointed at the cage. "You're going to die if you don't join us, Kirkland. You want to die?"

Kirkland didn't want to die. But he didn't

want to give in to Vinnie. Kirkland had made a lot of mistakes, but he wasn't black hearted like Vinnie.

"Sign on with Meat Hook," Razorback said. "You'll see. It's great. I'll put in a good word for you with the gang. They'll accept you the same way they accepted me."

Kirkland was about to reply when a gong rang through the camp. He looked up to see Meat Hook emerging from his hut. The bandit leader stood tall next to Bullet Head, the fat mutant with the steel helmet. They began to stride toward Kirkland's cage.

"This is your chance," Razorback replied. "I'll tell Meat Hook you want to join us. How about it, Kirkland?"

The dark-haired boy watched the mutants come closer. He didn't want to be like Vinnie, but he didn't want to die either. The choice was all too clear. He lifted his eyes and watched as Meat Hook drew closer to his cell. The iron hook was gripped tightly in Meat Hook's rough hand. He raised the hook and pointed it at Kirkland.

It was then that Razorback began to state his case for Kirkland joining the bandit army.

Three

Sir Charles Bookman stood on the deck of the schooner *Pacific* gazing toward the small harbor on the island of Papua. Sir Charles had been looking for his son Miles. The tall, aristocratic Englishman was studying the large speedboat that was moored to the pier. He wondered if the powerful vessel could help him in his search.

"Charles?"

The woman's voice came from behind him. He turned to see Katherine Wainwright standing on deck. She was Miles's mother and Sir Charles's ex-wife. They had met in Honolulu, joining forces in an effort to locate their missing son. So far they had been unsuccessful.

"Good morning, Katherine."

"What are you doing?" she asked.

Sir Charles gestured toward the speedboat. "I was just considering the possibility of hiring that craft to look for Miles."

Katherine nodded as she stepped up next to

him. "I've seen one of those before, when I guest-starred on that detective series that was filmed in Florida. What do they call them?"

"Cigarette boats," Sir Charles replied. "They're fast, even in rough seas. It might be helpful to search the islands the natives keep talking about."

Katherine frowned. "I don't like those stories, Charles. They're full of demons and devils. I hope Miles isn't trapped in a place like that."

Sir Charles took a deep breath. He believed the stories the islanders told about monsters from hell. He knew all about the experiments conducted by Cyrus Albright. Those experiments were the main reason that Sir Charles had been warned to stay away from the sector known as the Omega quadrant. Some of the warnings had been anonymous threats.

Katherine was staring at the cigarette boat. "I wonder who owns it?"

"A writer," Sir Charles replied. "At least that's what Johnny tells me."

He was referring to Johnny Kahana, a native of Papua. So far, he had been helpful to Sir Charles and Katherine. But Johnny was worried. His daughter Mae had been missing for over a week. He wanted to find her as much as Sir Charles wanted to find Miles.

"What kind of writer is he?" Katherine asked.

Sir Charles shrugged. "I'm not sure. Johnny

says his name is Andrew Stone. He writes thrillers, that sort of thing."

"Wait a minute," Katherine replied. "I read one of his books while I was on location. It wasn't bad."

"Have you ever met him?"

"No. I wonder what he's doing out here?"

Sir Charles shrugged. "Probably a recluse. Writers need solitude. I hope I can talk him into letting me hire his boat."

Katherine gazed toward shore. "Look, there's Johnny. I think he's coming out to see us."

They watched as a thin, older man boarded an outrigger canoe. He pushed away from the pier and started to paddle toward the schooner. In a few minutes, he was boarding their vessel.

"Top of the morning," Sir Charles said.

Katherine smiled at the bare-chested native. "Hello, Johnny."

Johnny offered a broad smile. He was missing a couple of teeth and his hair was thinning. He wore cutoff khaki trousers and tattered sandals.

"Are we leaving today?" Johnny asked.

Sir Charles grimaced. "I'm not sure, Johnny."

He frowned at the Englishman. "You said we were leaving today, to look for your son and my daughter."

"We're going to leave soon," Sir Charles replied. "I was just wondering if you could direct me to the chap who owns that boat."

Johnny turned to look at the sleek, red-and-white cigarette boat. "Oh no, Mr. Stone doesn't like to be bothered. No one ever goes to his place. He has a shotgun."

"I'm sure he'll listen to reason," Sir Charles offered. "I mean, the lives of our children are at stake."

Johnny shook his head. "No way, Charlie. Mr. Stone doesn't like anyone coming around. I can't take you there."

Sir Charles stiffened. "Then I'll go by myself."

"Wait!" Johnny cried. "You can't go. Mr. Stone will shoot you. He doesn't like people. He wants to be left alone."

Sir Charles turned, glaring at Johnny. "Look here, do you want to find your daughter or not?"

Johnny looked away. "Yes, I do."

"That boat may help us," Sir Charles went on. "If we're going to search those islands east of here, then we have to move quickly. I intend to find this Andrew Stone and ask him if he'll let me hire that boat. I know you want to find Mae, Johnny, so you're welcome to come along. If you'll help me, I'm sure things will go a lot smoother."

Johnny gestured toward the outrigger. "Okay, you win, Charlie. I'll take you to Mr. Stone."

They boarded the canoe and pushed away from the schooner. Sir Charles smiled and waved at Katherine. Johnny put the paddle in the water and began to guide the canoe back toward shore.

The harbor had come alive with activity. The mail boat was due in an hour, so the natives were preparing for its arrival. Sir Charles felt badly for Johnny and his people. They had been transplanted from an island where the military had conducted atomic tests in the early sixties. They were completely supported by welfare money from the government. But they were surviving as well as they could under the circumstances.

"I hope we don't get shot," Johnny said.

"I hope not," Sir Charles replied.

When they reached the pier, they climbed out of the canoe and started toward the village. Johnny had to stop to tell his wife where they were going. His wife protested in her native tongue. Sir Charles was certain that Johnny's wife had called him a fool.

Johnny came out of his house carrying a bag over his shoulder. "I'm ready, Charlie. You can still stop if you want."

"No, I want to keep going," Sir Charles replied. "What are you doing with the bag?"

"It's a long way," Johnny replied. "We need food and water."

"That far?"

Johnny started forward. "You can quit anytime you want. But let's get going. It'll be dark by the time we get there."

"Where are we headed?" Sir Charles asked.

Johnny pointed ahead of him. "There."

Sir Charles squinted toward the palm grove ahead of them. "The jungle?"

Johnny shook his head. "No, there!"

Sir Charles peered at the high mountain peak in the distance. It seemed to be a world away from the village. A ring of clouds surrounded the top of the volcanic ridge.

"Blast! We're going there?"

Johnny smiled weakly. "You want to quit now?"

Sir Charles drew a deep breath and shook his head. "No, Johnny, let's keep going. I'm going to find my son if it kills me."

"It probably will," Johnny replied.

They started forward, heading for the rocky shadow that stood like a colossus against the tropical sky.

Len Hayden paced back and forth on the beach, watching the southern horizon. It was almost midday. He felt badly about the things he had said to Miles, and he was sure that Miles would never forgive him.

Len kicked at the sand. It wasn't really Miles's fault that they had been marooned on the island. Len had just been feeling lost and alone. He wanted to go home to New Hampshire, to see his family, to live a normal life again. He could barely remember what it was like to sit down to a hot meal, to go to a movie, to watch a football game on Sunday afternoon.

"Darn it all!"

He kept his eyes on the horizon for a moment. It was stupid to watch for Meat Hook and his men. What could they do against the mutants? They could only hide from them and pray that they weren't found.

Len turned back, gazing toward the jungle. He wanted to apologize to Miles. He hadn't meant the things he had said.

Len walked up the path between the trees. When he reached the beginning of the path that led up to the lab, Len hesitated for a moment. What if Miles wouldn't forgive him? But he knew that he had to face the music even if Miles was still angry.

He climbed the path, stopping for a moment to drink from the stream. His heart was pounding as he came over the edge of the incline. He looked toward the lab, but he didn't see Miles.

Len walked across the yard, passing the barracks where the prisoners were kept during the experiments. He strode to the front door and entered the white building. Miles was sitting with his back to the wall.

Len grimaced and threw out his hands. "Bookman, I'm sorry. I was a real jerk. I didn't mean it."

Miles sighed and shook his head. "Don't sweat it, Hayden."

"No, I mean it. I'm really sorry."

"So am I," Miles replied. "I'm sorry about everything. Sorry we're lost on this island. Sorry that we're going to die."

"We've made it this far," Len replied. "Come on, we'll both stand watch. Nobody is going to kill us. We have to get back to school so we can tell everyone about this. Can't you see what old man Hauck will say when we write our themes for English class?"

A slight smile spread over Miles's thin mouth. "Yeah. 'What I Did on My Summer Vacation.' I got lost on a desert island, fought mutants, met a boy who ran with a dog pack. Who's going to believe us?"

"Who cares? Come on, let's go up top. We can watch for Augie."

Miles bounded to his feet, slapping hands with Len in a high-five. "Apology accepted, Hayden. We aren't finished yet!"

They hurried out of the lab building and climbed up to the roof. The sun was high overhead, casting a bright light on the sparkling ocean. Both of the boys looked out toward the water.

Miles's eyes grew wide. "Hayden, what's that?"

Len peered at the narrow canoe that knifed in the direction of their beach. "The mutants!"

"No," Miles replied. "It—it looks like Colgan!

And he's got somebody with him. They've got a boat!"

"Are you sure?"

"Look! He's come back."

They stood still for a moment, watching as the outrigger caught the waves. The boat surfed through the shallows, landing on the beach. Two figures climbed out of the craft. Len and Miles hurried down to meet them.

They flew across the yard, slipping sideways down the incline. Miles stumbled and rolled the last few feet to the bottom of the hill. Len helped him up and they tore through the jungle, heading for the beach.

When they emerged on the sandy stretch of shoreline, they were both out of breath. Colgan was coming toward them.

"Len, Miles! I made it back."

They stared at the slender figure that moved behind Colgan.

"Who's that?" Miles asked.

"A friend," Colgan replied.

Len gawked at the long hair and the red sarong. "I don't believe it!"

Miles's eyes grew wide. "It's a girl."

"This is Mae Kahana," Colgan said. "She comes from an island called Papua. I told you she was real, but you wouldn't believe me."

Four

Neil Kirkland's face was pressed to the bamboo bars of his cage. He had been watching the mutants all morning. Vinnie, or Razorback as he liked to be called, had taken his case to the others. They had gathered in a large circle in front of Meat Hook's hut, debating Kirkland's fate.

Kirkland felt a pain in his gut. If the bandits accepted him, he would have to join up. If they didn't accept him, he was going to die. It wasn't much of a choice.

Sweat poured down his face. He wasn't sure what to do. He knew he wasn't like Vinnie. His only crime had been to be truant from school, and he had once hit his history teacher. But Vinnie had stolen chapel poor boxes.

Kirkland's dark eyes watched the trial. Vinnie argued for letting Kirkland join the tribe. Meat Hook and Bullet Head listened.

One faction of the bandit army had gathered around to argue that they didn't want any more of the "children" among them. The children brought bad luck. The children should die for all the trouble they had caused.

The argument continued among the bandits until Meat Hook raised his iron weapon. Their voices trailed off. Kirkland pressed his face to the bars again, staring out at the bandits.

Meat Hook stood up and started for the cage. Bullet Head and Vinnie fell in beside him. The other bandits followed them.

When Meat Hook stopped beneath the cage, Kirkland knew that the moment of truth had arrived. He would either live or die.

Meat Hook pointed his iron hook at Kirkland. "Your brother Razorback has petitioned for you to join our ranks. Do you feel you are worthy?"

Kirkland's throat was so dry that he couldn't speak.

"Answer him!" Bullet Head cried. "Are you worthy to join us?"

The fear of death drove Kirkland to nod his head. He couldn't believe that he had done it. Joining them seemed better than dying.

Meat Hook smiled wickedly. "So, the child from Apocalypse Island thinks he is worthy to walk among the warriors of Lost Island."

Kirkland nodded again. The other bandits laughed at him. He hated them all. He wanted to kill them.

"Silence!" Meat Hook cried.

The laughter died immediately.

Kirkland watched as Meat Hook began to pace back and forth. This was a hideous nightmare. Kirkland wanted to wake up someplace else.

Meat Hook wheeled and pointed at Kirkland again. "No man comes to the brotherhood without a test of fire. Are you prepared to prove your loyalty to us, Kirkland?"

Kirkland glanced at Vinnie. The red-haired boy nodded. Kirkland's whole body trembled at the thought of signing on with Meat Hook.

"Answer me!" the bandit leader cried. "Are you ready to prove your loyalty to us?"

Kirkland heard his voice squeaking through the bars. "Yes!"

Meat Hook laughed loudly. Bullet Head grinned. What hideous task would they choose for him?

"What about your friends on Apocalypse Island?" Meat Hook asked. "Do you still want to help them?"

Kirkland grimaced. He didn't want to sell out the others. But he had to save his own life. He shook his head.

"Say it!" Bullet Head cried.

"No," Kirkland muttered.

"You don't want to help your friends?" Meat Hook asked again.

"No!"

Vinnie stepped forward a little. "See, I told

you he would come around. He hates them now. He wants to be with us. Don't you, Kirkland?"

Kirkland's eyes narrowed. He hated Vinnie. He was ashamed of himself for betraying the other boys. But he didn't want to face death.

"You want to be with us?" Meat Hook asked.

Kirkland nodded again. "I do."

Meat Hook glared up at him. "Then tell us where to find the other children."

"I don't know where they are," Kirkland replied. "They disappeared before you captured me."

A groan rose up from Meat Hook's men. They didn't believe him. They wanted his blood if he was going to lie to them.

"Kill him now!"

"He knows where they are!"

"Torture him until he tells the truth!"

"Silence," Meat Hook cried. "Kirkland, if you wish to join us, you must tell the truth. Where are the other children?"

A burning sensation filled Kirkland's chest. It was his life against the lives of Len, Miles, Augie, and Colgan. How could he sacrifice himself to save the others? It didn't make sense.

"Where are they?"

Kirkland lowered his head. "They're at the lab."

"Liar!" Meat Hook cried. "We were there. We didn't see them."

"They dug holes in the jungle," Kirkland replied. "When they saw you coming, they went into the jungle. They dropped down and hid in the pits. That's why you couldn't find them."

"He's lying," one of the bandits cried.

"Kill him!"

"He'll never be one of us!"

Meat Hook waved his iron scepter again to bring a hush over the camp. He looked up at Kirkland and nodded.

"He's telling the truth!" Vinnie cried. "It's just the kind of thing that the others would do."

Kirkland's hands were shaking. He felt terrible about ratting on the boys. At least he had bought some time.

"Tell us more," Meat Hook said. "Tell us all their secrets."

"Like what?" Kirkland asked.

Meat Hook's eyes narrowed. "What of the boy and the dogs?"

"Augie's nuts," Kirkland replied. "The dogs follow him like he was one of their own."

"Where can we find him?"

"I don't know."

Bullet Head pointed a thick finger at him. "Liar!"

"No," Kirkland said, "I mean it. One minute he's there, the next minute he's gone. He runs off into the jungle with those mutts. You never know when he's going to turn up."

"I believe him," Vinnie said. "I was there. I

saw Augie. Kirkland is right. The dogs are every-where and nowhere."

Meat Hook nodded. "Very well. You have told us much. But what of the pilot who landed on the island?"

"The plane is shot," Kirkland said.

"We know that," Meat Hook replied. "But where is the pilot? Is he with the other chil-dren?"

"I'm not sure," Kirkland told them. "I just know that Colgan lost it when Vinnie—I mean, Razorback hit him in the head with a rock."

Vinnie began to dance around in a circle. "See! I told you I beaned him! I put him out of commission. He's dog meat."

"He could be dead," Kirkland rejoined. "He wasn't there when I went back to the island."

It seemed to be getting easier to tell the mu-tants what they wanted to know. But Kirkland still fought the urge to tell them everything. He hoped they didn't ask him about the lab or the Proteus chamber. Even if he was saving his own skin, he didn't want the others to be locked up or killed.

"The hangar!" Meat Hook cried. "Did the children find a way in?"

Kirkland nodded. "Yeah, there was this plane. Only after Vinn—Razorback beaned the flyboy, nobody could fly it except me. So I stole it, but then we crashed because Razorback wanted to bring it here."

"See!" Vinnie cried. "I told you, Meat Hook. I wanted to bring that plane here, to serve my master."

Bullet Head grinned at the red-haired boy. "Your heart was pure, Razorback. Why did the plane crash?"

Kirkland saw a chance to get on Vinnie's good side for keeps. "It was Cruiser!" he cried, invoking the name of the boy who had died in the crash.

"Yeah," Vinnie chimed in. "Cruiser was the one. See, Kirkland wanted to bring the plane here, just like me. But Cruiser fought us. He was the one who made the plane crash."

Meat Hook's eyes narrowed and focused on Kirkland. "But *you* came here and freed Razorback from the cage. You were trying to get him to return with you to Apocalypse Island."

Kirkland thought he was sunk. Meat Hook had seen right through his masquerade. He knew Kirkland was just trying to save himself.

Vinnie stepped between Meat Hook and the cage. "That was in the past. Kirkland wants to join us now. I even have a name for him—Frankenstein."

"No way," one of the bandits cried. "He's not one of us."

"Kill him!"

"He doesn't belong on Lost Island!"

"Cut off his head!"

Again Meat Hook waved the hook and

35

brought their cries to a halt. "Listen to me, brothers. The child has given us information. If he has told the truth, then we should have no trouble returning to Apocalypse Island to find the children. We will bring them back here and let Frankenstein finish them off. Only then will we allow him to enter our ranks."

There was no argument from the bandits. They figured Kirkland would die sooner or later. They could wait for their bloodfest.

"I want to go back to Apocalypse Island," Vinnie cried. "I want to capture Len and Miles myself."

Meat Hook grinned at him. "Yes, Razorback. You will get the chance to prove yourself."

A cheer rose from the throng of bandits.

"You will return to Apocalypse Island with Bullet Head," Meat Hook announced.

Kirkland watched as the bandit leader moved toward the lagoon. Bullet Head was right beside him. The other mutants followed to help them.

Only Vinnie lingered for a moment, glaring up at the cage. "You better not be lying, Frankenstein!"

"I'm not, Razorback," Kirkland replied.

Vinnie ran off to join the others.

Kirkland leaned back, wiping the sweat from his face. He wasn't proud of what he had done. He just kept telling himself that it was better than dying.

* * *

36

Miles stared at the native girl. "Where did you come from?" he asked.

"From Papua," Mae replied.

"How did you get here?"

Mae took a deep breath. "I was out in my canoe one day, diving for oysters on the reef. Sometimes I find pearls. A storm blew up, and I couldn't get back to shore. The next thing I know, I was lost at sea. I had some water and a little food, so I was able to survive until I saw this island on the horizon. I guess I was lucky."

Len shook his head, frowning. "Maybe not. Things aren't that safe around here."

"I told her about Meat Hook," Branch rejoined.

"My people tell horrible stories about these islands," Mae went on. "Tales of demons and monsters. Supernatural things."

"They're true," Len said. "Only Meat Hook isn't supernatural. He's flesh and blood."

Miles turned to look at Colgan. "Branch, are you okay? You seem to be doing better."

Colgan sighed. "I can remember things. I know I'm in the Coast Guard. I'm a pilot. Hey, where are Kirkland and Augie?"

Miles looked at Mae again, not sure he wanted to upset her with the story of Kirkland's abduction. "They're gone. Mae, how far is it to your island?"

"Two days," she replied.

37

"Good," said Miles. "Maybe if we build another canoe, you can guide us there."

Soon they started back toward the lab. Colgan and Mae were famished. They entered the dense growth of the jungle and made their way in the shadows.

As they moved under the green vines, the birds and monkeys chattered overhead. Suddenly they heard something crashing through the jungle. In a moment a huge, gray dog was blocking their way on the trail.

"It's okay," Miles said. "It's only Commando."

Colgan cupped his hands and shouted into the jungle. "Augie, are you here?"

"Come out, Augie," Len cried. "It's only us."

Some vines rustled at the edge of the path. A small boy emerged from the jungle. He smiled at them and waved his hand.

"Hi, guys," Augie said.

The gray dog licked Augie's hand. Five more animals moved onto the path. The dog pack swirled around Augie.

Mae gaped at the dogs.

"This is Augie," Miles said. "He's our friend."

When Augie saw Mae, his eyes narrowed. "Who's this?"

"Mae Kahana," Colgan replied. "She came from an island west of here."

Augie smiled bashfully. "Wow, she sure is pretty."

Miles nodded in the direction of the compound. "Let's get going. Mae needs to eat something. Then we have to get back to the beach and hide that canoe."

"Canoe?" Augie said.

"Yes," Colgan replied. "Mae came here in an outrigger."

"Why do you have to hide it?" Mae asked.

Miles sighed. "Because I don't want Meat Hook to find it if—when he comes back."

Mae shuddered. "Meat Hook. What a horrible name!"

"You don't know the half of it," Len said.

Miles glared at him. "There's no need to scare her."

Len shook his head. "Looks like Miles has a girlfriend."

Miles blushed. "Shut up, Hayden."

"Come on," Colgan said. "Miles is right. We have to get back to hide that canoe after we eat."

They started toward the compound, with Augie and the dog pack leading the way.

Five

Sir Charles Bookman wiped the sweat from his brow. Ahead of him, Johnny Kahana walked between the trees at the base of the mountain. They had been traveling all day. Their trail had ended at another forest of thick growth that ringed the lower slopes of the volcanic ridge.

"Johnny," Sir Charles called. "Let's take a breather."

Johnny stopped and looked back at the Englishman. A strange expression had spread over his lined face.

"Sorry," Sir Charles said. "I only want to rest a moment. There's no need to look at me like I'm a—"

Johnny shook his head. "No, it's not that, Charlie." His gaze seemed to be fixed behind Sir Charles.

"What is it, Johnny?"

"I don't know," Johnny replied softly. "I have a funny feeling. Like someone is watching us."

40

Sir Charles peered into the shadows, not sure if he should trust the native's superstitious instincts. "How long have you had this feeling?"

"Since we left my village," Johnny replied.

Sir Charles suddenly felt a coldness on his spine. "How far are we from the place of this writer?"

"Not far."

"Do you suppose he's the one who's watching us?"

Johnny shook his head. "No. Well, maybe. But he hasn't been following us. He may be here, but this is something else."

"Evil spirits?" Sir Charles asked skeptically.

"Evil spirits don't make noise," Johnny replied.

Sir Charles pointed up the trail. "All of this talk is making me nervous. Let's push on."

They started up the trail again. As they ascended, the path began to grow darker. Johnny flinched at every sound and shadow. He kept stopping to peer into the undergrowth.

"What is it?" Sir Charles asked repeatedly.

Johnny turned toward the Englishman, frowning. "Let's go home, Charlie. We'll take your sailing boat and go to the islands."

Sir Charles squinted into the jungle. "Johnny, I don't see anything. I don't hear anything either."

"Please," Johnny said. "We don't need the

powerboat. We're wasting time if we want to find our children."

Sir Charles shook his head. "No, Johnny. I want to keep going. Perhaps this Stone chap can help us in a way we hadn't anticipated."

Johnny wiped the sweat from his forehead. He didn't say another word as he turned forward again. He began to walk up the trail. Sir Charles fell in behind him, trudging up the incline.

Johnny seemed to be moving faster in the shade. Sir Charles was not as quick. In a few minutes, he had almost lost sight of the little man.

"Johnny, please, wait for me!"

He started to take another step. Something in the jungle rustled. Sir Charles stopped for a moment. He turned toward the noise just as the dark figure leapt from the undergrowth.

A grim howling resounded through the jungle. Sir Charles saw the glinting of a knife blade in the narrow streaks of sunlight.

"No!"

Sir Charles lifted his hands, trying to defend himself. The knifeman fell on top of him, knocking Sir Charles to the ground. He looked up into the twisted face that was half-covered by a black mask.

His attacker brought the knife down. Sir Charles grabbed the man's arm, stopping the blade. The point of the knife hovered inches above his face, threatening to cut out his eye.

"Johnny!"

Suddenly the assailant cried out, as Johnny grabbed him from behind. He rolled off Sir Charles and leapt to his feet. Sir Charles quickly regained his balance, gawking at the intruder. The man was dressed in black, like a ninja warrior.

The intruder immediately made a slashing motion with the knife, trying to cut Johnny. Johnny backed away. Sir Charles's eyes focused on the glistening steel of the knife.

Johnny launched a rock, hitting the ninja in the shoulder. The man cried out and dropped the knife. The blade landed in front of Sir Charles.

"Get it!" Johnny cried.

As Sir Charles reached for the blade, the intruder also bent toward the ground. He touched the knife before Sir Charles. As he came up with the blade, Sir Charles grabbed his wrist. They began to struggle with the knife between them.

Johnny lunged again, but the ninja was quicker. He threw a back kick that caught Johnny squarely on the chin. Johnny fell to the ground, losing consciousness when he hit his head on the trail.

Sir Charles sent an elbow into the man's knotted stomach. The ninja barely grunted. Sir

Charles saw the knife inching closer to the bridge of his nose.

Bringing up his knee, Sir Charles smashed the attacker's stomach. The ninja cried out, and for a moment his body went slack. Sir Charles thought he had hurt him, but it was only a trick.

When the attacker relaxed, Sir Charles started to ease up. The ninja immediately stiffened again, slamming his elbow into Sir Charles's ribs. Sir Charles grunted and dropped to one knee.

A front kick hit the Englishman in the middle of his chest. The air left Sir Charles's lungs. He rolled backward, landing at the base of a palm tree. His chest burned. He couldn't move to defend himself.

The ninja hesitated for a moment, his eyes narrowing. It was as if he wanted to savor the kill. Slowly he raised the knife in the air.

Sir Charles lifted his hand but he was too weak. He knew the black-clad warrior was the last living person he would ever see. The knife blade started to fall toward his chest.

Suddenly there was a loud explosion in the jungle. The ninja's body buckled. He fell forward, landing on top of Sir Charles. Blood gushed from his back as he twitched and died.

When Sir Charles rolled the body off him, he looked up to see a man standing on the trail. The man held a smoking shotgun in his hands.

Sir Charles filled his lungs with air. "Andrew Stone, I presume."

The man moved closer. He was a short, stocky man with big arms and light blond hair. His rugged face scowled at Sir Charles. He had cold, steely blue eyes that were narrow and suspicious.

"Are you indeed Andrew Stone?" Sir Charles asked.

Suddenly the man bent low, putting the barrel of the pump-action gun against the Englishman's forehead. "I'm the one who asks the questions around here. Who are you?"

"Bookman. Sir Charles Bookman at your service, sir. Thank you for saving my life."

The man's brow wrinkled. "Bookman? The photojournalist?"

"One and the same."

The shotgun lifted from Sir Charles's forehead. "I've admired your stuff," the man replied. "Not bad."

"Are you Stone?"

"Yes, guilty as charged."

Stone looked down at the body of the dead man. Then he looked at Johnny Kahana, who was slowly getting to his feet. For a moment, Sir Charles thought Stone was going to shoot Johnny.

"He's my friend," Sir Charles said quickly.

Stone nodded. "I know Johnny. Did he bring you here?"

Sir Charles nodded. "I'm sorry if we're trespassing, but—"

Stone waved his hand. "Forget it. Who's the guy with the knife?"

"I was hoping you'd tell me," Sir Charles replied. "Doesn't he work for you?"

Stone shook his head. "Never seen him before."

"I wonder why he wanted to kill me."

Stone shrugged. "The evil that men do, eh. Come on, let me help you up. Are you strong enough to walk?"

Sir Charles nodded. "Yes, I think so."

Stone offered his hand, pulling Sir Charles to his feet. They both looked down at the bleeding body. The ninja twitched in the last stages of death.

Stone chuckled. "That double-ought buckshot really makes a hole. Lucky you weren't blown away yourself, Bookman."

Sir Charles grimaced at the huge hole in the assassin's back. "He certainly wanted me dead."

"Are you all right?" Sir Charles asked Johnny, who was now on his feet, rubbing his head.

Johnny gaped at the dead body. "What happened?"

"He attacked me," Sir Charles replied. "And I wish I knew why."

"Come on," Stone said. "Let's drag him up to my place and see what we can find out about him."

Sir Charles hesitated, squinting at the shotgun. "Your place?"

"Yeah, it's a half-mile up the mountain," Stone replied. "Don't worry about the hardware. I'm not going to shoot you. After all, we're both story tellers—one with words and one with photographs. That makes us brothers, sort of."

"Quite," Sir Charles replied.

Johnny gawked at Stone. "I told you he had a shotgun."

Stone laughed. "Yeah, but this is the first time I've ever used it on anyone."

"Allow me to commend your timing," Sir Charles replied.

Stone gestured toward the body. "Come on, let's get him up to my place. Maybe then we can find out why he tried to knife you."

The three of them bent down and picked up the body. It took them almost an hour to reach the recluse writer's house that had been erected on a ledge of the mountain.

"Home sweet home," Stone said. "I built it myself. Used the rocks from the mountain and clay from the jungle. Thatched the roof with palms."

"Nice place," Johnny said.

Stone winked at him. "Don't let the rumors fool you, Johnny. I'm really a nice guy. I started all that talk because I didn't want anyone bothering me."

"Rather ingenious," Sir Charles rejoined.

Stone nodded toward his house. "Come on, I'm anxious to see what this stiff has in his pockets."

They dragged the corpse onto a short porch in front of the house. Stone began to go through the pockets of the black clothing. Sir Charles sat in a wicker chair and watched him. Johnny hunkered down behind them, leaning back against the wall.

Stone labored for a few minutes, finally coming up with something in his hand. "Bingo! This may be what we're looking for."

He tossed a leather pouch onto a wooden table next to Sir Charles. Opening the pouch, he began to go through the contents. The assailant had been carrying money, a passport, and a lot of different papers.

Stone opened the passport. "Well, it says here his name is Joseph Smith. From Los Angeles."

Sir Charles examined the passport, too. "Probably a fake," he said.

"Whoa, what's this?" Stone exclaimed. "A business card."

"What's the name on the card?"

Stone squinted at the small writing. "Zach Donaldson. You know him?"

Sir Charles shook his head. "Donaldson? No, can't say as I do."

Stone's eyes grew wider. "Wait a minute! I know this guy. He's the aide for Senator Williams."

"Williams? From California?"

Stone nodded. "That's right. I had to do some research in Washington for one of my books. I called this guy once. He wasn't much help, but he did get me into the Library of Congress after hours."

Sir Charles leaned back. "Why would Senator Williams be involved in something like this?"

Stone held up a newspaper clipping that was several years old. "Maybe this explains it."

Sir Charles read the headline out loud. "Senate Approves Rehab Program for Hardened Criminals."

"What do you make of it?" Stone asked.

Sir Charles's eyes grew wide. "The Proteus Project! Williams has been behind it all along. That's why he doesn't want anyone going into the Omega quadrant. He's the one who's trying to stop me."

"Stop you from what?"

Sir Charles leaned forward. "Stone, I came here to ask you if I can hire that boat you've moored at the harbor."

Stone frowned. "My speedboat?"

"Yes. What would you charge me to lease it for a week?"

Stone shrugged. "Sorry, Bookman, it's not for rent."

"Blast!"

"But if you tell me what's going on, I might let you have it for free. I like a bit of adventure."

Sir Charles hesitated. He was not sure he could trust the writer, even if Stone had saved his life. He wanted the boat, however, so he really didn't have much choice. He had to take Stone into his confidence.

"It's a long story," he said. "And I don't have much time."

"Then talk quickly," Stone replied. "Before that ninja body starts to stink."

Sir Charles began to lay out the story for Stone. He explained how Miles had boarded a plane that later crashed in the area somewhere near Papua. He revealed that no one had wanted to help find the downed plane, save for one brave Coast Guard pilot who had also disappeared. The pilot had bucked his superiors to go looking for Miles.

"How come nobody wants to look around out there?" Stone asked.

Sir Charles explained the Proteus Project, the effort to develop a serum for criminals. The project had gone wrong, and the criminals had revolted against the scientists. There was every reason to believe that some of the criminals were still out there, living on the islands that had been deserted by the Proteus researchers.

"It's Senator Williams," Sir Charles went on. "That newspaper clipping proves it. Williams has been trying to stop everyone from coming out here. He doesn't want his mistakes to be uncovered. If the voters are told about the Proteus Project, Senator Williams's career will be ruined."

Stone shook his head. "Secret projects, capitol intrigue. It sounds like something from one of my books. It sounds *better* than one of my books. Are you sure about all this?"

Sir Charles sighed. "Mr. Stone, at the risk of being immodest, I am not without influence in certain circles. I called in every favor I had, including one from a general who benefited from a photo essay I created about him. But my efforts were in vain. While I was in Honolulu, I even received threatening calls that warned me to stop trying to find my son. I'm willing to bet those calls came from this Zach Donaldson. Senator Williams no doubt ordered him to put me off the trail."

Stone leaned back, folding his arms over his chest. "I think you've got a handle on it, Bookman. But look here, I've got a few connections around here. Why don't you let me see what I can do to help you?"

"No!" Sir Charles said emphatically. "I mean, I don't want anyone to know I'm here. There's been enough trouble already. I just want to find my son and go home. The best way for you to help is to let me hire your speedboat, Stone."

The writer shook his head. "It's not for rent."

Sir Charles stood up. "Then we have nothing else to discuss. Johnny, let's go."

"Hold your horses," Stone said. "I didn't say

you couldn't use my boat. I just want to make another kind of deal with you."

Sir Charles eased back into the wicker chair. "What kind of deal?"

Stone smiled at him. "You've got a heckuva story here, Bookman. And I'm interested in it."

"What are you proposing?" Sir Charles asked.

"Just this—I'll let you have my boat for free if you'll promise me exclusive rights to your story."

Sir Charles frowned. "That's a bit cold-blooded, Stone. After all, my son's life hangs in the balance."

Stone pointed a finger at him. "Don't forget, Bookman, I saved your life. That ninja would've sliced open your breadbasket if I hadn't shot him."

"You have me there," Sir Charles replied. "Very well, I don't suppose I have much choice. I agree to your terms. I'll exchange the rights for this story for the use of the speedboat."

"Now you're talking, Bookman!"

"Do you want me to sign anything?" Sir Charles asked.

Stone held out his hand. "I'm betting that you're a man of your word. Shake on it."

They shook hands to seal the bargain.

Sir Charles rose again from the chair. "Let's be on our way, Johnny. We don't have time to waste."

Stone waved his hand in the air. "I can help

you out there, Bookman. There's no need for you to walk back to the harbor."

"What are you talking about?"

"I have a trail bike in back of the house," Stone replied. "It's only a two hundred cc Honda, but it will get you back to the harbor faster than your feet. It'll carry you and Johnny."

"Thank you," Sir Charles replied. "I don't know how I can repay you."

"Just bring back a good story."

Sir Charles looked at the dead body. "What about *him*?"

Stone sighed. "Well, I guess this will just have to be our little secret. I can bury him where nobody can find him. There's no need to get the authorities in on this. I mean, he was trying to kill you. How about it, Johnny? We keep this to ourselves?"

Johnny nodded. "Fine by me."

Stone stood up. "Okay, you guys wait here. I'll get the bike for you. You do know how to ride a motorcycle, don't you, Bookman?"

"Quite," Sir Charles replied.

Stone went into the house. Soon they heard the sound of the motorcycle revving behind the house. In a few moments, Stone guided the vehicle around to the front. He got off and turned to Sir Charles.

"Here are the keys to the boat," he said. "If

you just run one of the engines, it'll be a lot easier on gas."

Sir Charles took the keys. "Thank you."

"Do you need weapons?" Stone asked.

"No, I brought my own," Sir Charles replied.

He had several automatic rifles on the schooner. Sir Charles wanted to be prepared. He wasn't sure what he would find when they reached the islands to the east.

"Be careful," Stone said. "I'll see you when you get back."

Sir Charles nodded and climbed onto the trail bike. Johnny sat behind him. Sir Charles put the bike in gear and they roared off down the mountain, leaving Stone to his burial detail.

In an hour they were back at the village. Sir Charles parked the bike near the speedboat. He climbed into the elongated vessel and cranked up the twin engines. The roar reverberated through the harbor.

"We'll need more gas," Johnny said.

Sir Charles nodded. He had several cans of fuel on the schooner. All they had to do was load them onto the cigarette boat.

"Do you want to say good-bye to your wife?" Sir Charles asked.

"I already have," said Johnny. "She always knows where I am."

Johnny loosened the tethers that held the boat on its moorings. They cast off and motored toward the schooner. Katherine was waiting on deck when they eased next to the sailboat.

"You did it!" she cried.

Sir Charles smiled. "We have to get her loaded quickly. I want to leave right away."

He threw a line to Katherine. She secured the cigarette boat. Sir Charles cut the engines. He and Johnny climbed on board.

They loaded everything they needed. Sir Charles also brought his binoculars and an extra compass in case the built-in compass failed on the speedboat.

When everything was loaded, he hopped down into the boat. Johnny was right behind him. Katherine came to the rail, as if she intended to board.

Sir Charles shook his head. "I'm sorry, Katherine, but you can't come with us."

Her face drew up in an angry expression. "Why not?"

"Well, it may be dangerous out there. And someone has to stay here in case —I mean, in the event that I don't come back."

She frowned, her anger turning to worry. "Oh, Charles. Please—"

He tried to smile. "It will be all right, Katherine. But if I'm not back in a week, go to that chap Stone. Tell him to do whatever he can to help find us."

"Charles—I—I love you!"

"I love you, too, Katherine. And I'll do everything I can to rescue our son. I promise you that."

"But, Charles, I think this is something we should do together. He is *our* son."

Sir Charles seemed to consider her reasoning for a moment. "I suppose you're right. Come on."

He cranked up the engines as Katherine boarded. Then Sir Charles gunned the throttle and headed out to the open sea.

Six

The afternoon shadows grew longer, deepening into evening shade over Apocalypse Island. Below the compound, the jungle was quiet. The birds and monkeys had retired from their feeding. The dull roar of the surf and the voices of the castaways were the only noises to disturb the tropical silence.

Len, Miles, Colgan, Mae, and Augie were sitting around a small fire. Commando was at Augie's feet, while the other dogs rested a few feet away.

Earlier, Len and Colgan had returned to the beach to hide the outrigger canoe that Mae had arrived in. The vessel had been secured in the rocks on the western tip of the shoreline. It was safe for the time being.

Len sighed and looked into the fire. "Well, here we are," he said. "Right back where we started, only with one more mouth to feed."

"Maybe not," Miles replied.

Colgan nodded. "At least we have the boat now. And we know that there's another island somewhere in this vicinity."

Miles looked at Mae. "How far is your island, Mae?"

She shrugged. "I don't know."

"Is it west of here?" Miles asked.

"I think so," Mae replied.

"She was lost in the storm," Colgan said. "She can't be sure."

They were quiet for a moment. Commando lifted his head to growl. Augie stroked the dog's fur.

Mae squinted at the wolfish animal. "Where did you get him, Augie?"

"The scientists left him behind," Augie replied. "I'm glad. Commando is the best friend I've ever had."

"He likes you," Mae said. "How did you tame him?"

"I pulled a piece of metal out of his foot," Augie replied. "We've been friends ever since."

Mae smiled.

Miles looked at Colgan. "Lieutenant, how are you feeling now?"

Colgan frowned, gazing into the fire. "I remember a lot of things. I know I went against orders to come here. My career is probably ruined. But at least I found you kids."

Mae yawned and stretched. She told the boys she wanted to lie down.

Augie stood up. "Come on, I'll take you into the lab. Commando and I will show you where to sleep."

Mae smiled. "Thanks, Augie."

She got to her feet. Before she left the fire, she walked over to Miles and kissed him on the cheek. Miles blushed and looked into the flames.

She walked away, following Augie into the lab building.

The others sat by the fire in silence. Mae's arrival had confused matters. They had to get back on track.

"We have to start making plans," said Colgan. "It's time to make a run for it."

Miles looked at the young lieutenant. "The outrigger?"

Colgan nodded. "It's our only chance."

"I was thinking the same thing," Miles replied.

Len looked at both of them. "The outrigger? That thing isn't big enough to take all of us."

"Yes it is," Colgan replied.

"There're five of us," Len said. "And what about Augie's dogs?"

"Augie won't go with us," Miles replied. "All along he's been saying that he won't leave the island."

"We have to make him go," Len argued. "Otherwise, we have to leave him here for Meat Hook."

Colgan looked at Len. "Do *you* want to try to force him to put those dogs in the outrigger?"

Len shuddered. "No, not really."

"And don't worry about Meat Hook getting him," Miles chimed in. "Augie won't be found by anyone unless he wants to be found. No, I think the four of us will fit in the outrigger. We can lay in supplies and head west to look for Mae's home island. We can send somebody back for Augie."

Len exhaled dejectedly. "Maybe you're right. I just don't like the looks of that canoe."

"Mae got here in it," Colgan offered. "We can make two more paddles. With four of us paddling, we might have a chance."

"I guess a chance is better than nothing," Len muttered.

Colgan gazed sternly at Len. "You understand we have to do something, Len. We can't stay here and wait."

"Yes," Len replied. "I understand."

"Then it's settled," Miles said. "We're leaving first thing in the morning in the canoe."

"We better get to work," Colgan said. "We've got a lot to do before then. We'll need food, water, and two more paddles."

"And we'd better take some kind of tarp," Len said. "Something to protect us from the sun."

"Good idea," Miles replied. "You're thinking now, Hayden. Let's get started."

As they moved to their tasks, Miles couldn't shake the odd sensation he had in his gut. It gnawed at him like a hungry rat, the feeling that they would never leave Apocalypse Island in the native canoe.

Neil Kirkland peered out of his cage, watching the bandit camp. Bright torches burned over the beach to ward off the darkness. The mutants were almost ready to launch the boat into the lagoon. Kirkland wished there was some way he could stop them.

Bullet Head and Razorback were going to Apocalypse Island on a commando raid. All day long they had been preparing for the sneak attack. Their bodies had been painted with weird camouflage. Len and Miles would never see them coming through the jungle.

Leaning back against the bars of the bamboo cell, Kirkland felt a pain in his stomach. He regretted telling the mutants about the hiding places that the boys had prepared on Apocalypse Island. When Bullet Head and Razorback found them, it would be Kirkland's fault. Their blood would be on his hands.

"Frankenstein! Hey, Frankenstein!"

Kirkland looked down to see Razorback standing under the cage. His body was covered with swirling black designs. He held a crossbow in his right hand. A long knife was tucked into his belt.

Kirkland sighed and gazed up at the darkening sky. "What do you want from me, Vinn—Razorback?"

"You're our brother now, Frankenstein. As soon as we return with the others, you'll be freed. We'll give you new clothes and you'll be one of us."

"I can hardly wait," Kirkland muttered.

"I hope you told us the truth," Razorback went on. "The truth will set you free, Frankenstein."

Kirkland felt a surge of anger inside him. But he held his tongue. He didn't want to make them angry. They would kill him if he did.

Razorback raised his crossbow in the air. "The brotherhood will live forever. Long live Meat Hook!"

"Frankenstein!" called a deep voice from the beach. Kirkland looked down to see Bullet Head. The fat man was also covered with dark camouflage.

Bullet Head pointed a finger at Kirkland. "If you didn't tell us the truth, Frankenstein . . ." He drew the finger across his throat. ". . . you're dead meat!"

Kirkland didn't reply.

Razorback laughed. "He told us the truth. Frankenstein is one of us now."

Kirkland winced. He had betrayed Len and Miles. How many times had Miles saved his life?

And Kirkland had repaid him by telling the mutants where to find him.

"We'll return with their heads!" Razorback cried.

I hope not, Kirkland thought.

Bullet Head and Razorback hurried to the catamaran that was already in the water. When they had boarded, the other mutants cheered and pushed them off. The catamaran sailed across the lagoon, disappearing in the night shadows.

"They're dead," Kirkland muttered. "Len and Miles are dead. And I killed them myself."

He stared up at the sky. He had sold them out to save his own life.

Seven

The cigarette boat was a blur of red and white on the smooth, blue water. Sir Charles stood behind the wheel, guiding the swift vessel toward the forbidden Omega quadrant. Johnny Kahana sat next to the Englishman and Katherine sat behind them.

They had been running due east since they left Papua. But there was still no sign of a land mass on the purple horizon.

Sir Charles eased back on the throttle. The boat slowed to a crawl. He finally cut the engine and gazed out over the smooth ocean.

Johnny stood up and peered into the distance.

"I don't see anything," Johnny said.

Sir Charles sighed. "Nor do I." He scanned the horizon through his binoculars.

"Let me try," Johnny offered, standing up.

But he couldn't see anything with the binoculars, either. The barren sea stretched before them, mocking their efforts to find their children. Still, they weren't ready to give up.

"Johnny?"

"Yes, Charlie?"

"Those islands your people were talking about—are you sure they're east of Papua?"

Johnny shrugged. "Maybe. That's what the stories say."

"How long have these stories been around?" Katherine asked.

"Long time. But they just started again a few years ago. Some say my cousin disappeared on one of the islands."

Sir Charles tried the binoculars again. He couldn't see anything, not even a sea bird. What if he was chasing some stale dream that had been passed down from generation to generation by Johnny's people? Miles might be hundreds of miles away.

"Something wrong, Charlie?" Johnny asked.

"Everything is wrong," Sir Charles replied.

Johnny peered toward the horizon again. "They're out there," he said softly. "I know it."

"What if they aren't? What if we're just blowing smoke?"

"Don't lose heart, Charlie. We have to keep going."

Sir Charles looked at the gas gauges. "Half full. I'll have to cut one of the engines. We can run on one for a while. We'll save fuel that way.

After all, we need to have enough to get back to Papua."

Johnny sighed and eased down into the cushioned seat. "Are we going to run all night?"

Sir Charles exhaled, looking toward the darkening horizon. "I suppose we shouldn't, but I feel like pushing on. We can run five or six knots, until morning. This thing has a spotlight on the front. We can flash it if we need to see where we're going."

Johnny cast a glance at the sky. "Going to be a good moon tonight. High and bright."

"I wish we'd see something," Sir Charles said. "Anything. Another ship, a bird. A fish. It seems so desolate out here, as if the gods of the sea are trying to warn us away."

Johnny reached back, picking up one of the automatic rifles. He took the weapon from its case and clicked a round into the chamber.

"Why are you doing that?" Katherine asked.

Johnny looked back at her, half-smiling. "In case the gods of the sea send us any surprises."

Sir Charles laughed a little. "I like your spirit, Johnny."

"Just make sure my spirit stays in my body," Johnny replied.

Sir Charles wanted to have one more look at the charts he had brought along. He scanned the maps in the dim light. But they were no good to him. There were no islands charted east of

Papua. If they kept going, it would be a blind search.

"What does the map tell you, Charlie?" Johnny asked.

Sir Charles shook his head. "Nothing useful."

"Johnny, have you ever seen those islands yourself?" Katherine asked.

Johnny took a deep breath. "Once, when I was a boy, my father took me fishing. We got lost in a storm. We found an island. It had mountains and jungles."

A shiver played across Johnny's narrow shoulders. He stood again, looking out over the ocean. He pointed to the east.

"We must keep going to our fortunes," he said. "We may not come back alive, but I know we will find what we are looking for."

Sir Charles nodded. "That's good enough for me."

Johnny sat down, holding the rifle on his lap. Sir Charles put the boat into gear. He inched the throttle forward. The boat began to move slowly toward the darkness to the east.

The white sail billowed in the tropical night breeze. Razorback sat on the deck of the catamaran, gazing into the darkness. He couldn't see anything ahead of the boat. He wondered how they were going to find Apocalypse Island without a light to guide them.

Razorback glanced backward over his shoulder. Bullet Head held the tiller of the catamaran. The fat bandit didn't seem worried about the darkness.

"How will we find the island?" Razorback called.

Bullet Head shrugged. "Don't worry about it. Just keep your eyes forward. Holler if you see anything."

Razorback looked toward the north again. His heart was pounding. He wanted the blood of Len and Miles on his hands. They had escaped the brotherhood too many times. Their luck had to run out sooner or later.

He clutched the crossbow tightly to his chest. His wicked imagination ran wild with ways to torture his enemies.

The catamaran knifed through the lapping water. Bullet Head held steady to the tiller. Razorback strained his eyes, but there was still no evidence of the island ahead of them.

"Where is it?" he cried in frustration.

Bullet Head grinned at him. "You're impatient for the kill, Razorback. I've taught you well."

"They have to die! I will vanquish all enemies of our master. Meat Hook will reign supreme!" Razorback shouted.

Bullet Head laughed. "Don't worry. They won't escape this time."

They sailed forward into the night. The red-haired delinquent kept his eyes on the horizon for a long time before the moon slipped into the sky.

A round, white orb began to rise overhead. The bright light reflected on the rippling ocean. They continued on for several hours before Razorback let out a blood-chilling cry.

He could see Apocalypse Island in the distance. The dark hump rose abruptly out of the sea.

"There it is, Bullet Head!"

The fat man nodded.

Razorback clutched the crossbow to his chest. It would be a while before he got to use it. The catamaran shot through the pale waves, heading straight for the sandy shoreline of Apocalypse Island.

Miles sat in a wooden chair in the lab basement watching Mae Kahana as she slept. He thought Mae was the most beautiful girl he had ever seen. He wished that she had not come to such a dangerous place as Apocalypse Island, but at the same time, he was glad he had met her.

The others were sleeping upstairs. Mae had been given the basement all to herself. Miles had come down to check on her.

Rising out of the chair, he moved next to the padded table. A lock of thick, black hair had fallen over Mae's face. Miles reached down to brush the lock away.

Mae stirred for a moment, opening her eyes. "Miles . . ."

"It's okay," he replied. "We've got the canoe loaded. We're leaving in a few hours."

Mae smiled and closed her eyes, slipping into her peaceful slumber. Miles took a deep breath. He watched her for another moment and then went upstairs.

Colgan's bunk was empty! Miles looked all around the compound, but found no sign of the pilot. He couldn't believe that he had wandered off again.

Walking around to the side of the lab, Miles climbed the narrow steps that led to the roof. He heard shuffling on top of the building. When he reached the roof, he could see a dark shape against the sky.

"Hayden?"

"Yeah, it's me," Len replied. "Who'd you think it was?"

Miles exhaled. "Well, I finished carving those paddles. Looks like we're finally getting off this rock tomorrow."

Len nodded. "I hope so."

"The only problem is that Colgan has wandered off," Miles said quietly.

Len shook his head. "Let's hope he knows what he's doing."

They sat quietly until something rustled below them.

They both looked down into the yard.

"It's only Commando," Len said. "He came outside."

Miles squinted toward the large, gray dog. "What's he doing?"

Commando stood in front of the doorway that led into the lab. He was looking toward the edge of the plateau. His ears were standing up.

"He hears something," Miles said, peering out at the reflection on the water. "Do you see anything?"

Len squinted toward the beach. "No. But it's hard to tell in the shadows. It looks like . . . I don't know. Is that . . . Bookman, what is it?"

From his pocket, Miles withdrew a small pair of binoculars that he had found in an old file cabinet in the lab. With the binoculars to his eyes, he studied the horizon. To the west, he saw something that broke the horizon line. Miles fiddled with the binoculars to get a better focus. It was a long, sleek boat that rode low in the water. There seemed to be three people in the boat. Was that his father standing at the helm, and his mother, her hair blowing in the breeze? He couldn't believe it. Was it a mirage? He looked again. It was real! Rescue was on the way! He fetched his notebook and wrote what he thought might be his final entry.

But in a few minutes, he was startled when Commando leapt up onto all fours. Soon, all of the dogs had joined him, barking at the night.

They weren't barking at what Miles had just seen. Something else was frightening them.

"Bookman, look to the south," Len cried. "The mutants are back!"

Eight

Razorback stood at the edge of the plateau. He could see the dim lights in the recesses of the laboratory. He started to take a step forward.

Bullet Head's strong hand grabbed Razorback's arm, stopping him. "Not yet, brother."

Razorback's face twisted into a horrible scowl. "Kill!" he hissed, waving his crossbow in the air.

"We have to take them the way we planned," said Bullet Head. "Listen. The dog is there. They have a pack of them."

Bullet Head hunkered down in the shadows, watching the lab. Razorback stood beside him. He held his crossbow tightly, watching for Len and Miles.

When Len and Miles reached the bottom of the steps, they stopped, gazing at Commando. The fierce gray dog had saved their lives before.

They had to take his barking as a serious warning.

Len peered toward the dark edge of the plateau. "What does he see out there? I can't see anything."

Miles shook his head. "I don't know."

The moonlight had cast an eerie pallor on the island. The shadows appeared to be swirling in front of them with phantom motion. Were those human figures or just tricks of the moonglow?

"I don't like this, Bookman."

"Neither do I. Where's Augie?"

"Right here, Miles."

The younger boy had been awakened by Commando's barking. He moved out of the lab, standing next to the gray beast. He rubbed the dog's ears, but Commando didn't look up at his master. His wolfish eyes peered toward the edge of the plateau.

"What is it, boy?" Augie asked.

Commando whined and paced nervously around his master. There was something out there that frightened him.

"Maybe we should go inside," Miles offered. "I want to make sure that Mae is safe."

Suddenly, Commando lowered his head. A deep growl rose from the back of his throat. He started to bark again.

Something moved in the jungle. They turned quickly to see Branch Colgan racing toward them.

"They're coming," Colgan gasped.

Suddenly, Commando broke away from them. The dog ran headlong through the moonshadows. He was attacking.

"No!" Augie cried.

Then a loud yelp echoed over the plateau. For a moment, there was silence except for a faint wimper in the distance.

Augie started to run after the dog. "Commando!"

Miles tried to grab him. "Don't, Augie!"

But Augie pulled away from Miles's grasp. He followed the same path taken by Commando. When he reached the edge of the compound, he gazed down at the motionless figure of his dog.

"Commando!"

Augie knelt down, touching the gray fur. He felt the wetness of Commando's blood. An aluminum arrow was protruding from Commando's body.

"No! He's dead! Commando's dead!"

Augie heard laughter above him. He glanced up to see the dark figure standing against the moon. He recognized the hateful tone.

"You!" Augie cried. "You killed my dog, Vinnie!"

"Razorback to you, punk. Yeah, I killed that mutt. And I'm glad I did. He had it coming."

Augie jumped to his feet. "You creep!" He charged straight at Razorback.

Razorback swung the butt of the weapon. He

caught Augie on the side of the head. Augie fell, blacking out from the blow.

Razorback took aim with the crossbow. "Good-bye, Augie. I'm going to pin your head to the ground."

A rough hand fell on Razorback's shoulder. "No!"

"Let me finish him off, Bullet Head."

The fat man shook his head. "Tie him up. We have to take him to Meat Hook. He will serve as sport."

"What about the others?"

"Don't worry," Bullet Head replied. "I'll take care of them."

Len, Miles, and Colgan had heard Augie's screams. They stood motionless for a moment. Augie's cries died away.

"We've got to hide," Miles said.

Colgan peered into the shadows. "I set some more traps, but it might not make a difference."

He looked down at the dog pack. They seemed to sense that Commando and Augie were gone. They whined and tucked their tails between their legs.

"Get 'em!" Colgan commanded, trying to put the dogs on the intruders.

But the animals turned away from the shadows. They wouldn't obey his order. Instead, they ran in the opposite direction, toward the mountain.

"We've got to get to our holes," Len said.

Miles nodded. "I'll get Mae."

"What holes?" Colgan asked.

"We dug pits in the jungle," Miles replied. "Two of them. Don't worry, there's room for everyone. Hayden, show Colgan. I'll see you down there."

He turned quickly, rushing into the lab.

Len started toward the right side of the compound. "Hurry, Colgan. While we still have time."

They ran for the edge of the plateau, where the escape ropes hung over the jungle. Len and Miles had devised the getaway route themselves. Below the ropes were piles of mattresses from the old prisoners' barracks.

Len grabbed the rope. "Swing out and drop. When you land, roll to the left. The pits are close by."

Colgan frowned into the dark jungle. "Are you sure?"

"I'll go first," Len replied. "Just do what I do."

Len took a deep breath. He braced himself and swung off the plateau. But as he flew out into the night, he felt the rope starting to give way. The rope broke, sending him out of control toward the jungle floor. He screamed all the way down.

Colgan stared into the black wall of vegetation. "Len!"

There was no reply.

Colgan started to turn back toward the lab. A huge figure loomed behind him. Thick hands closed around the lieutenant's neck.

"Now you're mine!" Bullet Head cried.

The fat bandit closed his grip on Colgan's throat. Colgan's eyes bugged out. He had to fight back. He kicked at Bullet Head, driving a foot into the mutant's groin.

Bullet Head grunted with the pain. Colgan dug his fingernails into the fat man's hands. Bullet Head loosened his grip for a second.

Colgan jabbed at his face, driving a thumb into Bullet Head's eye. The mutant screamed again. Colgan slammed his fist into the broad nose.

Blood poured onto the bandit's face. For a moment, Colgan thought he had a chance. But Bullet Head was too strong.

Colgan suddenly felt himself being lifted into the air. He cried out as Bullet Head spun him over his head like the propellor of a plane. Bullet Head launched him over the edge of the cliff.

Colgan fell like a rock, plummeting toward the dark floor of the jungle.

Miles hurried into the basement of the laboratory. Mae was still sleeping on the padded table. The noise from above hadn't awakened her.

Miles shook her. "Mae! Wake up! Hurry!"

Mae stirred from her slumber, looking up at Miles. "What's wrong?"

"We've got to hide," Miles replied. "The bandits have come back to the island. They're going to get us if we don't move fast."

A fearful expression spread over Mae's face. "Miles—"

"Just come with me," he told her. "We made hiding places in the jungle; we'll be all right."

Mae started to climb off the table. As she stood, she lost her balance, falling forward. Miles was able to catch her but she twisted her ankle.

"Ow, it hurts. I can't walk on it."

"Here," Miles said. "I'll help you. Put your arm around my shoulder. Hurry, Mae. We have to go."

"Where are the others?" she asked.

"They've already gone to hide."

Miles helped her toward the steps. Mae couldn't put any pressure on her ankle. They had to take the steps slowly, one at a time.

As they climbed the steps, Miles wondered if Mae would be able to take the fall into the jungle. It was a long drop in the darkness. She might be afraid to swing out on the rope.

"Come on, Mae," Miles urged. "We have to go faster."

They finally surmounted the top step, emerging in the upper room of the lab. Miles held the girl's weight as she hobbled. They were almost to the door when Mae looked up and screamed.

Miles lifted his eyes to the doorway. A dim figure stood in the threshold. Miles saw the glint of the arrow that was notched in the crossbow. The bow was aimed straight at them.

"That's far enough!" Razorback cried.

Mae was startled at the sight of the hideous teenager.

The color had drained from Miles's face. "Vinnie."

"My name is Razorback!"

Before Miles could reply, there was a rustling sound behind Razorback. Bullet Head pushed him out of the doorway. His fat face scowled at Miles and the girl.

"Good hunting, Razorback," the fat mutant said. "Looks like you bagged a buck and a doe."

"Let her go, Bullet Head," Miles said. "Take me, but don't hurt her."

Bullet Head grinned. "He's a knight in shining armor."

"Where are the other geeks?" Razorback asked.

Bullet Head drew a finger across his throat. "The flyboy and the other one are dead. I cut their little escape rope. They both fell."

Razorback lifted the crossbow again, aiming at Miles. "Then it's time for Bookman to join them."

"No!" snapped Bullet Head, shoving Razorback away. "We have to have our fun and games. We can't deprive our brothers of the spectacle."

A hellish grin spread over the face of the boy who had once been Vinnie Pelligrino. "Yes,

80

you're right. It's going to be a Lost Island Horror Show. You hear that Bookman? A real horror show. And you're going to be the star."

Miles put his arms around Mae Kahana. He hugged her for a moment before Bullet Head grabbed them and dragged them out of the lab. He couldn't believe that he was being captured and that Len and Colgan were dead. But he wasn't willing to give up. There *had* to be a way out of this predicament.

Razorback held the crossbow on them, herding Miles and Mae toward the beach. At the edge of the plateau, they picked up Augie, who was bound and gagged. Bullet Head threw the younger boy over his shoulder and carried him down the incline.

In a half hour, they were back on the beach. Bullet Head threw Augie, Miles, and Mae into the catamaran. The two bandits launched the boat into the surf. They lifted the sail, heading back to Lost Island with their prisoners.

Nine

Neil Kirkland opened his eyes when he heard the commotion on the beach. The mutants sounded happy. Cheers and catcalls rose in the night air.

Kirkland sat up, peering toward the lagoon. Torches burned brightly, and he could see a crowd gathering around a catamaran that had just sailed in to shore.

Bullet Head and Razorback had returned. From the sounds of the mutants, their mission had been successful. Then Kirkland saw Miles and Augie. At first he thought the third prisoner was Len. But then he saw the red dress and the long hair. Where had the girl come from? Kirkland watched as Meat Hook and Bullet Head dragged the prisoners toward the other cage that sat on the ground.

He knew he was responsible for their capture and because of that he was saved. But he couldn't shake off his feeling of guilt. Once again he had betrayed the others.

Meat Hook and Bullet Head pushed their captives into the other cage. They raised the bamboo cell over the beach, cranking it up on the rope. Miles, Augie and the girl swung a few yards away from Kirkland.

"Frankenstein!"

Kirkland looked down at Razorback, who stood below his cage.

Razorback laughed. "We did it, Kirkland! We got them. All thanks to you. Now Meat Hook will set you free."

"Yes!" the bandit leader cried. "Our brother Frankenstein is one of us. He has proven himself."

Kirkland looked down at the hideous face that stared at him. Meat Hook was smiling. Bullet Head reached for the mechanism that would lower Kirkland's hanging cage.

"No!" Kirkland cried. "I'm not one of you!"

Meat Hook frowned at him. "What's wrong, Frankenstein?"

"My name isn't Frankenstein," Kirkland cried. "And I'm not one of you! Miles is my friend."

"Shut up!" Razorback yelled.

"You all belong in hell!" Kirkland shot back.

Razorback took a step toward the cage. "Do you realize what you're doing?"

Kirkland shook his head. "I don't care. I can't

be like you, Vinnie. I'm not a monster. I'm not Frankenstein."

Razorback turned to Meat Hook. "Sire, he doesn't know what he's saying. Let him go so I can talk to him."

Meat Hook scowled at Kirkland. "What's your problem, Frankenstein?"

Kirkland shouted at the bandit leader. "I'm not one of your followers. You're a madman!"

A collective groan spread through the camp. Kirkland had committed the worst crime. He had shown disrespect for Meat Hook.

"Kill him!" someone cried.

"Death to the infidel."

"He blasphemed the name of Meat Hook."

Meat Hook waved his iron claw in the air. "Silence! Frankenstein has spoken. He has made his choice. Now he will pay the price with the others."

"Pay the price, pay the price," the mutants chanted hungrily.

Meat Hook laughed loudly. "You will regret the words you have spoken."

"Kill him now!"

"Spill his blood!"

"No," Meat Hook cried. "He will keep. We must let him grow stronger with the others. I want them in perfect health when they pay the price."

"Pay the price, pay the price."

"To your huts," Meat Hook commanded. "We

will begin to prepare in the morning. Our ceremony will take time. We must be ready."

The mutants began to move away from the cages. Only Razorback lingered, glaring up at Kirkland.

"You blew it," Razorback said. "I had the others ready to accept you. You really blew it big time, Kirkland."

"Drop dead, Vinnie."

Razorback wheeled away, heading for his hut.

Kirkland turned to look at the other cage. Miles was sitting up. He stared across the way at Kirkland.

Kirkland sighed deeply. "I'm really sorry, Miles."

"Did you help them?" Miles asked.

Kirkland looked away in shame. "Yes, I'm afraid I did. But I won't join them, Miles. I can't."

Miles shook his head. "Great," he said blankly. "Now we can all die together."

The cigarette boat chugged slowly through the dark waves. Sir Charles kept his eyes on the compass, making sure their course was due east. In the seat next to him, Johnny Kahana slept soundly, while Katherine dozed in the back.

A dim glow had begun to brighten over the ocean. The sun was finally rising. They had run all night at the low speed.

Sir Charles checked the gas gauge. They still

had three eighths of a tank. Even if they didn't find the islands, they could make it back to Papua if they ran on one engine.

"Where are you, Miles?" Sir Charles said under his breath.

The light on the horizon continued to get brighter. Sir Charles held the wheel steady. Johnny stirred on the seat waking to the cool dawn. He sat up and peered toward the orange horizon. He rubbed his eyes for a moment.

"Nothing yet," Sir Charles said.

Johnny stood up, grabbing the binoculars. He scanned the ocean for signs of land. He finally lowered the binoculars and shook his head.

"It doesn't look good, Charlie."

"I know, Johnny. Let's keep going for another hour, and then we can decide what to do."

The boat churned forward. Rippling waves lapped against the hull. Johnny kept watching with the binoculars. The hour was almost gone when Johnny dropped the lenses and let out a whooping howl.

"What is it?" Katherine asked, waking up abruptly.

Johnny handed her the binoculars as she stood up. "See for yourself."

Katherine lifted the lenses to her eyes and then passed them to Sir Charles. His heart began to pound when he saw the shape on the horizon. It looked like a dark triangle jutting up out of the ocean. At first he thought the shape might be clouds. But as they drew closer, he knew that it was unmistakably land.

"We made it," Johnny said.

"That remains to be seen," Sir Charles replied as Katherine squeezed his shoulder hopefully.

But he still gunned the engine and raced for the island in the distance.

Len Hayden opened his eyes, staring into blackness. His whole body ached from the fall he had taken. He hadn't landed on the cushioned mat that he and Miles had rigged. Instead, he had crashed through the vines and branches, slamming onto the hard ground.

The blackness before him was the rich earth of the jungle floor. Len tried to move. The pain was sharp, but he was still able to sit up. When his eyes focused, he looked around the jungle, trying to remember what had happened.

"Bullet Head!" he said to himself.

The mutants had come to attack them. But what had happened to Miles and Colgan? Had they been captured or killed? Had Mae and Augie been taken alive?

Rising to his feet, Len stood on wobbly legs. He had to get out of the jungle. But where would he go? What if Bullet Head was still on the island?

Len stopped for a moment. He thought he had heard something. The jungle was quiet. He took a few more steps before the low moaning reached his ears.

"Who's there?" he called.

The moaning continued, getting louder. Len turned in a circle but he couldn't see anything in the jungle.

"Where are you?"

"Up here," came the faint reply.

Len lifted his eyes to the ceiling of the jungle. He saw the lump in the vines above him. Branch Colgan had landed in the branches of a tropical tree.

"Help me down," Colgan said.

"What happened?" Len asked.

"The fat man," Colgan replied. "He threw me off the plateau."

"Hold on, I'll get you down, Branch."

Len took his time climbing the tree. His arms and legs were sore, but he still managed to reach Colgan. He dislodged the lieutenant from the branches. They were able to climb down slowly.

"They really got us," Colgan said when they were on the ground. "That fat one picked me up and spun me over his head."

"That's Bullet Head," Len replied. "I think he cut the rope that I used to swing out. It broke on me."

Colgan peered upward. "We're lost down here. I wonder if the others are . . . I don't hear anything. Maybe they got away."

Len shuddered. "Maybe they didn't."

"Come on, let's get out of here."

They began to walk through the dense undergrowth. In Len's addled state, nothing looked familiar to him. But they finally reached the stream that ran down from the mountains. Len knew how to make it back to the compound from the stream.

Colgan bent down, drinking from the clear water. Len also drank and washed his face. When they were finished, they waded in the stream, following it until they had cleared the jungle.

Colgan stopped at the base of the plateau, gazing upward. "I wonder if they're still here?"

Len took a deep breath. "Do you want to find out?"

Colgan shook his head. "No. Let's go. We can grab the outrigger and head out to sea."

"What if they're wounded up there?" Len asked.

"Do you think the bandits would stay here?"

Len shook his head. "No. They'd take them back to Lost Island."

Colgan turned toward the beach. "If we hurry, we might be able to find help before it's too late." He started down the path.

Len fell in behind him. He wondered if Miles was still alive. He had seen Bullet Head's rounded steel helmet before. Had he crushed Miles's skull?

They emerged from the jungle, walking onto

the beach. They headed for the outrigger's hiding place, but they never made it. Both of them looked up when they heard an engine's noise rolling over the water.

"A boat!" Len cried.

Colgan squinted at the red-and-white vessel. "I don't believe it."

They both began to wave their arms, screaming loudly to get the attention of the three figures who rode in the long, swift watercraft.

Ten

"Look!" Katherine cried. "On the beach!"

Sir Charles gazed toward shore for a moment. He quickly lifted the binoculars to his eyes. As soon as he saw the two figures waving at him, he turned the speedboat toward the beach and gunned the throttle.

The red-and-white vessel roared into the surf. Sir Charles cut the engines. The hull of the boat coasted into the shallows, lodging in the sand.

Sir Charles jumped out into the ankle-deep water. Johnny and Katherine were right behind him. They ran to meet Len and Colgan.

Sir Charles grabbed Colgan's arms. "Lieutenant, you made it here."

Colgan smiled. "Yes, but I'm afraid I crash-landed."

"Sir Charles!" Len cried. "How did you find us?"

"It doesn't matter now," the Englishman replied.

91

"Where's Miles?" Katherine asked. "He's my son," she added, nodding to Colgan.

Len hesitated. "I—I—"

Johnny stepped up next to Sir Charles. "Have you seen my child?"

Colgan squinted at the smaller man. "Who's this?"

"Johnny Kahana," Sir Charles replied. "He's been helping me. He's also been looking for his daughter."

"Mae," Colgan said.

Johnny's eyes grew wide. "Then you've seen her?"

Colgan nodded. "Yes."

"Where is she?" Johnny asked.

"And Miles," Katherine rejoined. "Where is Miles?"

Len began to tremble. "I don't know."

"What do you mean you don't know?" Sir Charles demanded. "Is he here?"

"He was," Len replied. "But now we don't know what happened to him." He was scared to tell Sir Charles what he *thought* had happened to Miles.

"The bandits attacked us last night," Colgan said. "We think they may have—well, we aren't sure—"

"My daughter!" Johnny cried. "Is she dead?"

"We don't know," Len replied. "We just don't know."

* * *

Shortly after sunrise, the bandit camp began to come to life. The bandits staggered out of their huts and filed past the huge cauldron where a new cook stirred the bubbling repast. Miles wondered what had happened to the one called Cannibal. But he wasn't going to ask about him.

Mae and Augie sat in the cage next to Miles. Mae had gone into shock. She seemed to be in a trance, some kind of waking coma. Augie was scared. Like Miles, he watched the mutants cautiously. Miles woke up knowing that what he had seen through the binoculars from the laboratory roof hadn't been a mirage. Every hour since then, he had been thinking about what he had seen. Somehow, in his sleep, his subconscious mind had told him that his parents really were here to save him. But could he save them from the mutants first?

"What are they going to do to us?" Augie muttered.

Miles sighed. "I don't know, Augie." *Whatever it is,* he thought, *it can't be good.*

When the bandits had eaten their breakfast, the cook turned toward the cages. He offered the prisoners bananas and dried fish on the end of a stick. Augie and Miles grabbed the food and began to eat. Miles tried to offer food to Mae but she wouldn't take any.

"Is she all right, Bookman?" Kirkland called.

Miles looked over at Kirkland, whose face was pressed against the bamboo cage. Kirkland had already eaten his breakfast. He was curious about the girl.

"Where did she come from?" he asked.

Miles glared at Kirkland. "What do you care?"

"I do care," Kirkland replied. "I mean it."

Miles sighed. He was angry at Kirkland, but he really couldn't blame him for what he had done. Kirkland had been confused. He had probably been trying to save his own life when he gave the bandits information about them.

"I'm sorry, Bookman," Kirkland pleaded. "I made a mistake."

Miles didn't reply. At least he knew that Kirkland hadn't joined the mutants like Vinnie. That was something. And if they were going to escape, they might need Kirkland. He was strong and quick, even if he wasn't too bright.

"She came from an island west of here," Miles replied. "Her name is Mae. She showed up on Apocalypse Island when her canoe was lost in a storm."

"What about Len?" Kirkland asked. "And the flyboy?"

"Bullet Head said he killed them," Miles replied. "They're gone."

Kirkland lowered his head. "Sorry."

"Kirkland, is there any way out of here?"

"Forget it, Bookman," the voice said from below. "You're not getting out of here. You're dog meat."

Miles looked down at Razorback's hateful scowl. "Good morning, Sunshine. How are things in the Twilight Zone?"

Razorback glared up at him. "You won't be so smart when you have to play the game, Bookman."

"Yeah? What game is that?" Miles asked.

"The Wages of Sin," Razorback replied.

Augie put his face against the bars, glaring back at Razorback. "Vinnie, I'm going to get you for killing my dog."

"You aren't going to get anyone," Razorback cried. "You suckers are dead. Get used to the idea."

Razorback turned and walked away. He joined the other bandits who were starting to build something in the middle of the camp. It looked like a large platform was being raised in the sand.

"What's that?" Augie asked.

Miles sighed. "An altar."

"For what?"

"For the sacrifice," Miles said. "And we're going to be the offering."

"Where is Miles?" Sir Charles asked again.

Len shook his head. "I told you, I don't know."

95

The Englishman looked at Colgan. "Tell me what you *do* know, Lieutenant."

Colgan exhaled. "The bandits came last night. They attacked us. They tried to kill Len and me by throwing us off the plateau."

"Plateau?"

Colgan pointed back toward the mountains. "Up there. The compound where the scientists conducted their experiments."

"The Proteus Project," Sir Charles said.

Len frowned at him. "You know about it?"

"Yes. But that's not important now. What did they do with Miles? Did they kill him?"

Colgan shook his head. "We aren't sure. We had been planning to leave in the outrigger that Mae brought. Four of us were going to head out this morning, and try to get back to Papua. Augie was going to stay."

"Augie?" Katherine asked.

"He was with the delinquent kids we picked up in Majoru," Len replied. "Kirkland was captured or killed. Vinnie joined the mutants. Some of the others were killed."

Sir Charles gazed toward the mountains. "You say this compound is up there somewhere?"

Colgan nodded. "We didn't go back there because we were afraid of what we might find. The mutants might still be around."

Sir Charles looked up and down the beach. "I don't see any boats. We're going up there to have a look. Johnny, get the weapons. Katherine, stay here."

"No. I'm coming with you," she replied defiantly.

Sir Charles began to argue but then stopped.

Johnny waded back to the boat. He hopped in and grabbed the three automatic rifles. When he had given the rifles to Sir Charles, he went back to anchor the cigarette boat on the beach.

Sir Charles tossed one of the rifles to Colgan. "I hope you know how to use this."

Colgan smiled. "If I had one of these last night, those outlaws wouldn't have had a chance."

When Johnny came back onto the beach, Sir Charles gave him one of the rifles. They were armed and ready to explore the plateau.

"What about me?" Len asked.

"Stay here," Sir Charles replied.

Len shook his head. "No way. I'm going with you."

Sir Charles started to protest. "Len, you can't—"

Colgan stopped him. "Sir Charles, Len has been a good soldier. I trust him to do the right thing. He's not a kid anymore, not after what he's been through."

Sir Charles sighed. "Very well. But you'd better stay behind us, Len. You too, Katherine."

Colgan started forward. "I'll lead the way."

They walked across the beach, entering the

jungle on the narrow path. They trudged through the shadows and the thick under-growth. As they went higher on the trail, Colgan had to warn Sir Charles and Johnny about the mantraps.

Sir Charles stopped, gawking at the pit-and-spike snares. "What have you come to on this island?"

"Incredible," Katherine whispered.

"It's been life and death," Len replied. "But Miles has been great, Sir Charles. He's never been afraid. He always had a plan. He was doing fine until—well, until last night."

"Keep going," Sir Charles replied.

Colgan led the way toward the compound. They climbed the incline, emerging on the flat ground. There they saw the dead body of Commando lying in the dirt. The arrow protruded from his body.

"We should bury him," Len said. "He was a good dog."

Sir Charles had an expression of disbelief on his thin face. "What is this? Where did this animal come from?"

"The scientists left him," Len replied. "They were using dogs in their experiments. Augie befriended Commando. They were buddies."

Johnny Kahana was staring at the two buildings. "What kind of place is this?"

"An evil place," Colgan replied. "You don't even want to know what went on here."

Sir Charles waved his hand. "Spread out. Let's see if they're still here. Be careful."

They all started forward, afraid of what they might find. Johnny and Len searched the old prisoners' barracks but came up empty. They joined Sir Charles, Katherine, and Colgan in the lab.

They hadn't found anything on the upper floor. All five of them descended into the basement, which was empty. Len triggered the secret chamber with the password, Proteus, but it was also vacant.

Sir Charles squinted into the shadows of the hidden compartment. "Food, water, and gasoline. They thought of everything."

"That's how we've been able to survive," Len said.

"We can use the gas," Johnny Kahana rejoined.

Colgan sighed with relief. "Well, they're not here."

"They took our children," Katherine said. "But where?"

"There's another island south of here," Len replied. "They call it Lost Island. The mutants went there after they fought the scientists."

Sir Charles turned toward the stairs. "Then we have to go there immediately."

"Hold up," Colgan said.

"We haven't any time to waste," Sir Charles replied.

"I agree," Colgan said. "But we do need a plan. We can't go rushing in there like wild men. We need to talk it out first."

"Yes, you're right," Sir Charles replied. "But let's make it quick."

They all sat down in the basement to hash out a course of action.

"How many of these bandits are there?" Sir Charles asked.

Colgan shrugged. "Thirty, maybe more. Forty tops."

"Do they have weapons?"

"Yes," Len replied. "Crossbows and knives."

"No guns?" Johnny asked.

Len grimaced. "A few. I know Meat Hook has a rifle."

Katherine gaped at him. "Meat Hook?"

"That's the leader," Len went on. "He has this iron hook that he carries around with him."

"This is a nightmare!" Sir Charles cried.

Colgan shook his head. "You haven't seen anything yet. Listen up, Sir Charles, there are some choices we have to make here."

"Such as?"

"We've got the boat out there," Colgan replied. "Somebody could go for help. We can face those mutants alone, but it's going to be tough."

Sir Charles shook his head. "I'm not parting with the boat. That's our way out of here. Besides, I've tried to enlist the aid of virtually everyone I know, but no one has been willing to help."

Colgan looked at Johnny. "What about your island? Is there anyone there who can help us?"

Johnny rubbed his chin. "My people are brave. But I don't know if I could talk them into coming to these islands. They have always been afraid of the magic here."

"Can't blame them for that," Colgan said. "It's not even magic, and I'm scared to death."

"What are we going to do?" Katherine asked impatiently.

"Do you want to save your children?" Colgan asked.

"You know we do," the Englishman replied.

"Then we need to send somebody for help," Colgan said. "The odds are stacked against us. We need an ace in the hole."

"But we've only got one boat," Sir Charles said.

Colgan held up two fingers. "No, you're forgetting about the outrigger. I could go in that and take it to the west. If I could reach Papua, I might be able to round up some kind of help."

Johnny stared at him. "You? What do you know about navigating?"

"I'm a pilot," Colgan replied. "And I can paddle that outrigger."

Johnny shook his head. "No. If somebody is going to leave in the canoe, it should be me."

"Then you'll do it?" Colgan asked.

"No," Johnny replied. "I'm not leaving as long as my daughter is here."

"I could do it," Len offered.

Colgan leaned back, shaking his head. "No, you can't."

"Why not?"

"Because you're the only one of us who's been to Lost Island," Colgan replied. "You know the layout. Can you find the bandit camp?"

Len nodded. "Yes, we can go through the jungle. We did it before. The mutants didn't even know we were there."

Colgan looked at Sir Charles. "What about it, Sir Charles?"

Sir Charles sighed. "You're right, Colgan. We should send someone for help in the outrigger. Although I wonder if anyone will respond. And if they do, will they find anything here but our dead bodies?"

"I'll do it," Colgan said.

Johnny shook his head. "No."

"But—"

"I'll do it," Johnny replied. "I'm the only one who can make it back to Papua in the outrigger."

Sir Charles looked at the native man. "You don't have to go, Johnny. But if you do, I promise I'll do everything within my power to save your daughter. I swear it."

"Are you going to Lost Island?" Johnny asked.

Sir Charles looked at Colgan. "Lieutenant?"

"We can reconnoiter," Colgan replied. "But I'm not sure we'll be able to attack them."

"If my son is in danger, then we'll attack," Sir Charles said coldly. "I don't care about my own life. But I intend to save the lives of our children if I possibly can."

Colgan gestured toward the secret chamber. "Then let's get ready. We can start by filling the tanks of that boat."

They gathered the remaining cans of gasoline and started for the beach. When they reached the water's edge, they filled the tank of the cigarette boat. Colgan and Len then helped Johnny launch the outrigger from its hiding place in the rocks.

Johnny sat in the canoe, lifting the paddle. He cast a final look over his shoulder. He dug the paddle into the ocean.

Eleven

Len couldn't believe the speed of the red-and-white boat. The pointed hull knifed over the clear, smooth water. Sir Charles had the bow directed due south, toward Lost Island.

The engines groaned under full throttle. Sir Charles stared grimly ahead as he guided the vessel. Branch Colgan held the automatic rifle tightly. Katherine was quiet, but alert. They weren't sure what they would find. But Len knew firsthand the horrors that awaited them at the hidden lagoon where Meat Hook reigned.

Len's eyes grew wide when he saw the dot of land growing bigger on the horizon. The cigarette boat had made it in less than an hour.

As they drew closer, the boat began to bounce in the choppy waves created by the inshore currents. Sir Charles throttled down, and the engines whined. Sir Charles stared at the narrow spit that jutted out from the beach.

"Do you know where we are?" he asked Len.

Len nodded and pointed to the low-peaked mountain that sat beyond the shoreline and the bordering jungle. "We're at the northern tip of Lost Island. Miles and I climbed that mountain once."

"Where are these bandits?"

Len pointed to the south, along the coast. "There's a hidden lagoon on the southern end of the island. It's guarded by high rock cliffs. A channel leads through the rocks. They're camped on the beach of the lagoon."

"What's behind them?" Colgan asked.

"Jungle."

"Can we get to the camp through the jungle?" Sir Charles asked.

"Yes," Len replied. "We've done it a couple of times."

Sir Charles looked at Len. Was this really the boy who had befriended his son? Len had been a schoolboy; now he was talking like a combat veteran. Sir Charles had to wonder what kind of shape Miles was in.

"What do you think, Sir Charles?" Colgan asked.

Sir Charles sighed. "Well, I'd like to get a look at the camp. I'd like to know if Miles is there, and if he is, whether or not he's alive."

"We'll have to beach the boat," Colgan said.

"There are bays in these rocks," Len replied. "We could anchor it in one of them."

Sir Charles shook his head. "No, I want to be

able to launch it quickly. I'm going to put it on the beach."

Sir Charles gunned the throttle. The boat soared toward the sand. As they coasted in, Sir Charles raised the propellors so they wouldn't scrape. The vessel slid easily onto the beach.

Sir Charles immediately jumped out and secured the boat with an anchor rope. Colgan grabbed the rifles and climbed over the side. Katherine started to follow them.

"No," Sir Charles said. "I want you to stay with the boat, Katherine. I'm not risking you against these madmen."

Katherine hesitated but didn't argue. "Please be careful," she whispered.

Len came over the rail, landing on the beach. "I know the trail through the jungle."

Sir Charles looked at Colgan. "What do you think, Lieutenant?"

Colgan shrugged. "I think Len can handle it. He's got guts. Your kid has guts, too, Bookman. Miles is a real top gun."

Colgan threw Len one of the rifles. "Do you know how to use it?"

Len pointed to the slide. "Pull this back to load it. Safety here. Squeeze the trigger. Always keep it pointed toward the ground unless you're going to use it."

"Come on," Sir Charles said gravely. "I want to find my son. Let's get moving."

They started for the jungle with Len leading the way.

Johnny Kahana dug the paddle into the ocean, propelling the canoe to the west. He wished he had stayed behind, although he knew that the Englishman was right. Someone had to go for help if the demons were as bad as the boy said.

Johnny's eyes squinted toward the horizon. He wondered how long it would take him to get back to Papua. They had run the distance in the boat in a day and a night. The boat had gone slowly for a great deal of the time, but the Englishman had covered some of the distance at top speed. It might take Johnny three days to do it in the canoe.

He dug the paddle into the sea, praying to the gods that had always watched over his people. He had to make it back to Papua. Especially if he wanted to see his daughter alive.

Len stopped when he heard a strange sound ahead of them. They had been walking through the jungle all day. The trek had been slow in the heat and the dense vegetation.

Sir Charles stepped up next to Len. "What is it?"

"Listen," Len said.

Colgan came around on the other side of Len. "It sounds like—like hammers."

Len dropped low suddenly, hitting the dirt belly down. "We have to crawl from here."

Sir Charles and Colgan also dropped to the ground. They began to crawl toward the sounds of the hammers. The bandits seemed to be building something in their camp.

The three of them slid under the vegetation to the edge of the sand. They got close enough to see the hanging cages. Sir Charles saw Miles looking out through the bars. He wanted to call to him, but then he caught a glimpse of the fat man walking through the camp. He must've weighed three hundred pounds. A rounded steel helmet covered his head.

Colgan also gaped at Bullet Head. Neither of them had ever seen such a spectacle. All of the other bandits were dressed in a similar fashion —combat boots, ragged leather vests, torn pants. Their bodies were covered with tattoos and primitive decorations.

Len studied the platform that was being erected in the center of the camp. What were the bandits going to do with Miles? Kirkland, Augie, and Mae were also prisoners. Why hadn't Meat Hook killed them yet? Maybe he had something worse in mind.

Sir Charles began to crawl backward, away from the camp. Len and Colgan followed. They retreated to the deepest part of the jungle, where the bandits couldn't hear them talking.

"Who was the juggernaut in the steel helmet?" Colgan asked immediately. "He's the one who came after me."

"Bullet Head," Len replied.

"I wonder what they're building?" Sir Charles said.

Len grimaced. "Meat Hook and his men aren't exactly normal, Sir Charles. In case you haven't noticed. They do all kinds of weird things. It's probably some ritual."

Colgan patted his rifle. "I'll give them some ritual."

"Maybe later," Sir Charles replied. "One thing in our favor—if they're planning something big, they probably won't be leaving the lagoon."

"What're we going to do?" Len asked.

Sir Charles was silent for a moment before he replied. "We have to be ready to strike. And the time must be right. We'll hide out here, keeping watch on the camp. There's no need to move until we're sure that Miles is in danger."

Colgan nodded. "I'll go back to the boat, lay in some supplies, and make sure Katherine is safe."

"Good man," Sir Charles replied. "We may have to wait awhile. Let her know that everything is okay."

Five days later they were still in the jungle outside Meat Hook's camp. Sir Charles was determined to wait for just the right opportunity to rescue Miles.

"They still haven't done anything," Len said to Colgan. "What gives?"

Colgan exhaled tiredly. "Well, the kids are still alive. Even Kirkland. We're still kicking, too."

Len shook his head. "I'm getting tired of this. Why won't Sir Charles let us try to free Miles?"

"Because he wants his kid alive. He—whoa, what's that?"

Colgan peered into the jungle. He could hear the noise. Something was coming toward them.

They both hunkered low in the brush. After a moment, Sir Charles came into their hidden camp. He knelt low next to them.

"Any change?" Colgan asked.

Sir Charles shook his head. "Same as yesterday. That platform is finished, but they haven't done a thing."

Colgan started to crawl away. "I'll take my shift now." He disappeared quietly into the jungle.

"Miles okay?" Len asked.

"Yes, he seems to be getting on. It pains me to see him in that cage. But I'm afraid I'll lose him if we move now."

Len leaned back against a palm tree. For five days, Sir Charles and Colgan had been watching the camp, alternating six-hour shifts. They had made a resting place deep in the green shadows where the bandits couldn't find them. They wouldn't let Len take a shift. He was in charge

110

of checking on Katherine, running supplies from the boat, including food, water, and a five-gallon can of gasoline. Sir Charles had insisted on bringing the can of fuel.

"The one you call Meat Hook keeps watching the sky," Sir Charles said to Len. "Could you venture a guess as to why?"

"He's waiting for something," Len replied. "Who can say what he's waiting for? It's got to be crazy."

"I've counted thirty-one of them in all. Not good odds. Any sign of Johnny today on the horizon?"

"No, sir."

Sir Charles grabbed the canteen and drank deeply.

Len took a deep breath before he spoke again. "Sir Charles, I want to take one of the watches on the mutant camp."

"No, Len."

"Why not?"

Sir Charles smiled a little. "Because I won't have your parents getting mad at me for letting you get killed."

"But—"

"Enough," Sir Charles replied. "Get some rest."

"Yes, sir."

Sir Charles reclined on the ground, dropping off immediately into a deep slumber. Len tried to nap, but he couldn't get to sleep. He watched the shadows grow longer in the jungle. It would be dark soon, time for Colgan to return to their hiding place.

Sure enough, Len heard the rustling sound in the undergrowth. Colgan came back with a wide-eyed look on his face. He seemed to be frightened.

Sir Charles sat up and looked at him. "What is it, Lieutenant?"

"Get your guns," Colgan replied. "I think it's about to happen."

"What?" Len asked.

"The mutants," Colgan said. "I think they're about to do something to those kids. They're on the move, Bookman. It's now or never."

Twelve

Miles gazed out nervously at the bandit camp. Some of Meat Hook's men were putting up torches all around the big platform that had been erected. They were getting ready for something. Miles knew it would be something bad.

"What are they doing?" Augie asked.

Miles shook his head. "I don't know."

Mae put her hand on Miles's shoulder. "I'm afraid, Miles. I don't like these men. They're going to hurt us."

Miles tried to sound reassuring. "They haven't hurt us so far, Mae. We might get lucky."

"No," she replied. "We're going to die. I can feel it."

Augie glared at the red-haired teenager who approached their cage. "I'm going to fix him for killing Commando."

Razorback walked past their cage, heading for Kirkland's hanging cell. He stopped on the sand, looking upward, offering Kirkland one more chance to join the mutants. Kirkland refused.

Razorback shook his head. "It's over for you, Kirkland. You could've been Frankenstein. But now you'll only be dead."

Meat Hook and Bullet Head approached the twin cages. They stopped next to Razorback.

Meat Hook raised the point of his hook. "The heavens are right. The stars are positioned. You, Kirkland, will face the challenge."

"That's right," Bullet Head added. "Tonight you'll play *Wages of Sin*. You must pay the price."

Kirkland looked down at them. "You mean I get to go out fighting? Great. What about Miles and Augie? And the girl?"

Meat Hook smiled wickedly. "None escape the challenge. You must all play *Wages of Sin*. It is decreed."

"Let the girl go," Kirkland pleaded. "You don't have to kill her."

Meat Hook laughed. "You're right! She'll be more use to us alive. We need a new cook. She can learn our ways. All must pay the price. Now lower their cages. It is time for the game to begin."

Sir Charles clung tightly to the automatic rifle, gazing into the evening shadows of the mutant camp. He was close enough to hear Meat Hook's command.

Len and Colgan were right beside him, bellies to the earth. Len wondered if he could actually shoot someone with the rifle. But then he saw Miles being lowered to the beach. He had to do what was required to save his friend.

Colgan looked at Sir Charles. "What now?" he whispered.

"We have to create a diversion," Sir Charles replied. "And we have to be quick about it."

"You have a plan?" Colgan asked.

Sir Charles nodded. "We have to draw back first."

They crawled away from the camp to their hiding spot.

"Now this is how it unfolds," Sir Charles said quickly. "Listen very carefully. We can't afford to make a mistake."

Augie screamed when Bullet Head tried to pull him out of the cage. He grabbed Bullet Head's fat fingers and sunk his teeth into the flesh. Bullet Head immediately cuffed Augie on the side of the head, rendering him senseless for a moment. He then dragged the younger boy onto the sand.

Razorback grinned at Augie. "How's your mutt? Did he go to doggie heaven?"

Bullet Head dragged Augie away, toward the platform.

115

Meat Hook came after Miles. Mae grabbed his arms, screaming for Meat Hook not to take Miles away. The bandit leader yanked Miles away from her grasp, jerking him from the cage.

Miles didn't resist. He was afraid that Meat Hook would hit him. He wanted a clear head. If there was one chance to get out of this horror, Miles hoped he would be able to spot it.

"Miles!" Mae cried from the cage.

Meat Hook closed the door to the hanging cell. He commanded Razorback to raise the cage again. *At least they're not going to kill Mae*, Miles thought.

The bandit leader put the point of his hook on Miles's throat. He pulled Miles across the sand to the spot where Bullet Head waited with Augie. A long stake protruded from the ground. Miles and Augie were tied to the stake, back to back with their hands behind them. They were both trembling.

A drum began to bang somewhere in camp. Meat Hook and Bullet Head left the boys tied to the stake. Miles watched as they moved back toward Kirkland's cage. They began to lower it to the beach.

Miles looked to both sides of him. The jungle was on the right, the platform to the left. Miles peered into the darkness of the thick undergrowth. The jungle would be the way to go if they got a chance to flee.

But there didn't seem to be any hope. Meat

Hook and Bullet Head pulled Kirkland from the cell. They dragged him toward the platform that was bathed in torchlight. Kirkland was led onto the platform and then thrown down.

Meat Hook and Bullet Head left the bizarre stage. They were replaced by a weird-looking man in white-face. He wore the tattered shreds of an old tuxedo. A joker's leering grin was drawn around his mouth in red paint. When he spoke, his voice rang eerily deep and forceful.

"Gather round," the white-faced man said to the bandits. "Hurry, you don't want to miss the show."

The throng of mutants ringed the platform, shuffling for a good view of the festivities. As they crowded in, the host turned quickly to kick Kirkland in the ribs. Kirkland grunted and rolled around in pain.

Miles shook his arms, trying to wriggle out of his bonds. "Augie, see if you can work your hands free."

The eerie voice pealed through the camp. "And now it's time to play *Wages of Sin*, Lost Island's number-one game show."

The mutants cheered and made animalistic noises.

"What is *Wages of Sin*?" the emcee asked.

"Death!" the mutants cried in unison.

The host turned to regard Kirkland. "Now here's our first contestant. His name is Neil Kirkland, but you might have called him Franken-stein if he had joined our merry troupe."

"Boo!"

"Frankenstein must die!"

"Some grand prize," Miles muttered as he struggled with his bonds.

Augie grunted and sweated on the other side of the stake. "They're too tight, Miles. I can't break free."

Miles lifted his eyes to the stage. "Better check this out. Looks like we're going to be next."

The white-faced host made a sweeping gesture over the mutant horde. "We can't play our game with only one contestant. So now I'd like to introduce our second player. He hails from Lost Island. He's not a graduate of the Proteus Project, but rather a convert to our convict cause. Please give a hearty Lost Island welcome to the one, the only—Razorback!"

The crowd parted and suddenly Razorback stood alone under the torchlight. His face was drawn up in an expression of disbelief. The host extended his hand toward the red-haired delin-quent.

"We're waiting for you, Razorback!"

"Me?" he said weakly. "Why me?"

Bullet Head leaned in, giving Razorback a long machete. "He is of your past, brother. You must finish him to complete the bond."

Razorback looked at the weapon and smiled. "Sure. Sure," he said weakly.

Bullet Head began to lead the cheer. "Raz-or-back! Raz-or-back!"

Razorback threw himself onto the stage. Kirkland immediately jumped to his feet. He had recovered from the kick in the gut.

Razorback waved the machete at him. "Come on, Kirkland. Let's see what you can do against this." He started to stalk Kirkland with the long blade.

Miles held his breath, rooting for Kirkland. He saw Razorback make the first lunge with the machete. Kirkland managed to elude the swing of the weapon.

"Come on, Kirkland!" Augie cried.

Razorback began to swing the machete, trying to hit Kirkland in the head. Kirkland was quick enough to get out of the way. He danced around the platform until a gnarled hand came from the crowd, tripping him.

"No!" Miles cried.

"Cheaters!" Augie yelled.

Kirkland lay on the platform, motionless. Razorback lifted the blade over his head. He brought it down toward Kirkland's chest. Kirkland rolled out of the way as the blade sunk into the platform. The point of the machete lodged in the wood. Razorback struggled to pull it free.

Jumping to his feet, Kirkland seized the opportunity to kick Razorback in the chest. Razorback staggered backward. Kirkland threw several hard punches that caught Razorback squarely in the face. Blood began to pour from his nose.

"Get him, Kirkland," Augie cried.

Kirkland slammed a fist into Razorback's gut. The red-haired bandit went down on one knee. Kirkland hit him in the head, knocking him flat on the stage.

A hush fell over the bandits. Kirkland ran to get the machete. But when he reached for the knife, a mutant hand grabbed it and pulled it away.

"Dirty cheaters!" Augie railed.

Kirkland went after Razorback again. But the bandits had already pulled him off the stage. They were giving him water and rearming him with the long blade. When Razorback had recovered, the mutants lifted him back onto the platform.

"Nice try," Razorback said. "Now it's your turn, Kirkland."

He started to swing the machete again. Kirkland was able to avoid the sharp blade for a while. But the mutants weren't taking any chances this time. They finally tripped him and held him pinned to the platform, holding him there.

Razorback hovered over Kirkland with the machete. "Good-bye, sucker."

"No!" Miles cried.

Razorback lifted the blade over his head. But he never brought it down on Kirkland. The jungle seemed to explode suddenly. Rising balls of flame lifted toward the sky like jets from hell.

The mutants all turned to view the unexpected blaze. Meat Hook and Bullet Head were agape. They forgot about Kirkland and the others. They stared at the wall of fire that spread through the vegetation.

Miles and Augie were wide-eyed at the swirling flames. The whole jungle seemed to be ablaze. Who had started the orange inferno?

"What's happening?" Augie cried.

Miles didn't reply. He had a feeling that he knew. Suddenly he saw shadows against the fire. Someone was running toward him.

On the platform, Neil Kirkland jumped to his feet. He hit Razorback, knocking him down. When Razorback fell, Kirkland grabbed the knife and leapt off the stage. He ran toward Miles and Augie, cutting their bonds with the sharp edge.

The mutants began to scramble, looking for their weapons. Shots rang out under the torchlight. Some of the bandits fell in their tracks. Others dived to avoid the gunfire from the automatic rifles.

"Miles!"

Miles turned toward the familiar sound of the voice. "Father!"

Sir Charles grabbed his son, embracing him

for a moment. A crossbow twanged in the shadows, sending an arrow into the stake where Miles had been tied. Colgan stepped up next to them and fired his rifle, killing the bandit who had shot the arrow.

"Let's run!" Sir Charles cried.

He started to pull Miles toward the jungle.

"No!" Miles cried. "Mae! We have to save Mae!"

Kirkland hurried toward the hanging cage. He cut the rope with the machete. The cage crashed to the ground. He pulled Mae from the wreckage and threw her over his shoulder, carrying her toward the jungle. Colgan followed, covering his rear.

Miles looked back to see Len helping Augie. But Augie didn't want to go. He was trying to wrestle the rifle from Len's hands.

"Augie!" Len cried. "We have to go."

More arrows flew threw the night air. But Augie was determined. He finally freed the automatic rifle from Len's hands. When he had the gun, he turned toward the platform where Razorback was climbing to his feet.

"You killed Commando!" Augie cried.

He lifted the rifle. A look of terror seized Razorback's face. He started to back away, to run. But it was too late. Augie squeezed the trigger. A hail of bullets pelted Razorback's chest. The red-haired boy fell dead in a pool of gushing blood.

Len grabbed Augie, pulling him away from the mutants. The arrows continued to fly. Len ran toward the fire, joining the others at the edge of the jungle.

"We'll never make it through there!" Kirkland cried.

Sir Charles pointed to a narrow corridor between the flames. "We left a passageway. Stay in the shadows. We'll make it."

"Good thinking, Dad!" Miles cried.

Colgan went first, leading the way. Kirkland came behind him, carrying Mae. Sir Charles and Miles followed with Augie and Len in their tracks. They receded into the jungle, splitting the wall of flame.

The mutants weren't far behind them. They gave chase, running between jets of fire. Colgan turned back once or twice to fire his rifle, trying to drive back the rushing mutants.

As they moved deeper into the jungle, the flames began to die. Soon they were running in darkness. They held on to each other so no one would get lost. They could hear the bandits close behind them.

But they were not caught. They managed to reach the beach before the mutants set upon them. Katherine, hearing the commotion, had the boat revved up and ready to go. They were able to jump in the cigarette boat and take off in a matter of seconds.

When they were in deeper water, Sir Charles

cranked up both engines. He gunned the throttle. The boat roared away from the beach as the mutants burst onto the sand. A few arrows flew toward the boat, but it was already out of range.

"We did it!" Colgan cried.

Katherine embraced Miles and quickly kissed her ex-husband, who stood at the helm, guiding the boat through the night. The cigarette boat flew across the open sea. The Englishman didn't turn to look at his son, who gazed up admiringly.

"Good show, Dad!"

"Hey, Bookman!" Len cried. "Bet you never thought you'd see us again."

Miles slapped hands with Len. He turned to slap hands with Kirkland. He turned and hugged Mae.

"Are you all right?" Miles asked.

"I think so," she said. "I just want to go home."

The boat continued on at full throttle for another thirty minutes. But then they all heard a clicking in the engines. After a moment, the clicking turned into a whir. Suddenly a noxious puff of smoke came out of both engines. The speed boat sputtered and died.

Everyone froze as the boat drifted in the darkness.

"What happened?" Augie asked.

Sir Charles tried to start the engines but they wouldn't turn over.

"We blew a gasket," Kirkland said. "Maybe I can fix it."

"In the dark?" Colgan asked.

Kirkland sighed. "Let me see if I can lift this engine cover."

They all watched as Kirkland tried to tinker with the engines. Sir Charles managed to produce a flashlight. But it wasn't enough. Kirkland said he needed tools.

The boat drifted for a long time before they heard the waves crashing ahead of them. Apocalypse Island rose up out of the sea. They managed to land the boat on the beach, pulling it to safety.

Kirkland immediately broke into a run, heading for the compound. Len and Colgan went with him, dragging back every tool they could find. Kirkland began to work on the engine by the glow of the flashlight. But by the time the sun began to rise, he hadn't fixed it.

"I'm almost there," he said confidently.

"Almost isn't good enough," Sir Charles replied. "Look!"

They all turned to the south. The horizon was covered with the sails of the bandit fleet. Meat Hook and his men were approaching in the purple pallor of daybreak. They were still far away, but growing closer to Apocalypse Island with each hopeless moment.

Thirteen

Sir Charles looked away from the approaching fleet, gazing up toward the hidden compound. "We can retreat. Find a place to hide."

Branch Colgan was rummaging through the boxes of rifle cartridges. "We've got plenty of ammo. If we can find a place where they can't reach us, we might be able to hold them off."

"Meat Hook isn't going to get me again," Augie cried. "I'm going to find my friends."

"No, Augie!" Len cried.

Augie broke for the jungle. His short legs carried him over the sand at a rapid clip. Sir Charles and Colgan also cried out for him to stop, but he kept going for the rain forest.

Sir Charles nodded to Len. "Try to catch him."

Len started after Augie but he could not reach him before Augie disappeared into the thick undergrowth. Len would never be able to find him in the jungle. He just hoped the dog pack accepted Augie *without* Commando to protect him. Len turned and ran back to the boat.

Sir Charles and Colgan were still frozen in the boat. Kirkland labored over the twin engines with his wrenches.

Colgan peered out at the sails. "They'll be here in ten minutes."

Sir Charles started to get out of the boat. "We'll have to take our chances on the higher ground."

"No!" Kirkland cried. "I think I've got it. Try the ignition switch now. Go on, see if it works."

Sir Charles reached back, turning the ignition key. The engines sputtered and then roared to life. Kirkland had fixed them.

Len jumped in the air, waving his fist. "Yes!"

"Good work, Kirkland," Sir Charles said.

Colgan jumped out, putting his shoulder to the hull. "Let's launch this baby and get out of here."

Sir Charles waved at Miles. "Put the girl in here."

Miles led Mae to the rail of the boat. Sir Charles lifted her in. She sat on the cushioned seat, with Katherine close beside her.

Miles joined Len and Colgan on the hull. They started to push. Kirkland also leapt over the side to help them.

The cigarette boat eased back into the water. The engines were a little irregular. As soon as

127

they were floating, Kirkland jumped back in to make adjustments. The rhythm of the motors became smoother under his touch.

"Can we go?" Sir Charles cried.

"Yeah, but take it easy at first," Kirkland said. "Ease into it. We've got a small gas leak back here. I don't want to the whole thing to vapor lock and blow sky high."

Len, Miles, and Colgan came over the side, flopping in the boat. Katherine sat next to Mae, comforting her. Len, Miles, and Colgan picked up rifles, watching the white sails that grew larger in front of them.

"Don't fire yet," Colgan ordered. "They're out of range."

Sir Charles eased the throttle forward. "Here we go!"

The cigarette boat began to move through the shallows. Sir Charles kept inching the throttle toward a higher speed. Kirkland stood over the engines, watching them closely.

"Easy, Bookman!" he cried.

Sir Charles looked over his shoulder. "They're getting closer!"

The mutant fleet swung out in a wide arc, trying to cut in front of the speedboat. Sir Charles turned forward. He couldn't wait any longer. He needed a burst of velocity to outdistance the bandits.

"I've got to try it," he called.

Kirkland grimaced. "Don't—"

But Sir Charles gunned the throttle. The red-and-white vessel shot forward, throwing everyone off balance. The hull knifed through the waves. For a moment, it appeared that they would get away.

A puff of smoke from the engines dashed their hopes. Smoke swirled around the back of the boat. The vessel came to a halt offshore. They were drifting helplessly in front of the mutant fleet.

"I told you not to dog it!" Kirkland cried.

The current caught the boat, pushing it toward the western tip of the island. Kirkland picked up his tools again. If he couldn't fix the engines, they were going to be sitting ducks for Meat Hook and his men.

"They're getting closer!" Len cried.

Miles jumped up and grabbed the other rifle. "Let's shoot them!"

Colgan was already aiming at the catamaran that led the mutant armada. "They're almost in range."

The bandit vessels also rode the tidal surge. They were heading for the tip of the landmass. Colgan fired a couple of shots, but the bandits were smart enough to stay out of range.

"They're trying to cut us off!" Colgan cried.

Sir Charles gazed back at the beach. "We've got to get ashore again. Use the butts of the rifles for paddles!"

They tried to paddle the heavy vessel, but

they couldn't budge it against the current. When they peered to the west again, they could see the mutants' boats curving around in front of them.

Colgan pointed his rifle at the bandits. "This is it."

They drifted closer, heading for the last showdown with Meat Hook. Kirkland didn't give up on the engines. He kept working until he finally raised his head and cried out.

"Try it now!" he hollered. "Give it the—argh—"

They glanced back to see Kirkland wrestling with himself. An aluminum arrow was lodged in his chest. The shaft had come from the mutant fleet.

Len, Miles, and Colgan started to fire their rifles. Some of the bullets hit home. Several bandits fell from their catamarans, screaming. The others shifted their sails and tillers, ready to retreat from the barking of the rifles.

"We can't hold them forever," Colgan cried. "They'll pick us off slowly."

"Help me!" Kirkland muttered as he slumped to the floor of the boat.

Sir Charles knelt beside Kirkland. But there was nothing he could do. The arrow was lodged deeply in his chest. Blood gushed from the red circle.

"They're coming in again!" Colgan cried.

But the bandits never came within shooting

distance. They seemed to veer off at the last minute. Their boats circled away from the disabled vessel.

"What are they doing?" Len said.

Miles shook his head. "I don't know. Playing with us."

Suddenly Mae cried out. She had jumped to her feet. Her finger was pointing toward the smooth waters on the western shore of Apocalypse Island.

"Look!" she cried. "They have come back!"

Miles turned and immediately smiled. "All right!"

"Yeah!" Len cried.

Sir Charles gazed over the side. "I don't believe it."

"Who are they?" Miles asked.

"Johnny Kahana," Colgan replied. "Mae's father. And it looks like he brought a lot of his friends."

Outrigger canoes and power boats stretched in a broad line across the water. Johnny had made it back to Papua. He had rallied his people to help him rescue his daughter.

"Father!" Mae cried.

A small speedboat roared out of the native fleet. Johnny Kahana and Andrew Stone approached the cigarette boat. They pulled alongside to help the others. They lifted Kirkland first, carefully passing him to safety.

Mae went next. The others followed, abandoning the red-and-white vessel. The smaller boat moved back toward the line of native boats.

Sir Charles looked at Stone. "You came, too?"

The writer grinned. "I wouldn't have missed this for anything."

"Look!" Colgan cried. "They're coming again."

They all peered back to the south. Meat Hook was launching an attack. His boats were trying to swing in on the natives.

Johnny shook his fist at them. "You won't get away with it."

The native vessels shot forward to meet the bandits. Arrows flew from crossbows, falling in front of the natives. But the residents of Papua had come prepared. Suddenly the air was full of exploding rifles. The mutants sailed straight into a wall of lead.

Screams rose in the air. The mutants fell off their boats, dying in the water. Some of them tried to pull back, but it was too late. The rifles cut the masts from their boats. The ones who weren't killed were left to drown in the ocean.

"Where did you get those rifles?" Sir Charles asked.

Andrew Stone smiled. "AR-Fifteens. I had them at my place. I like to be prepared for anything."

"Look!" Miles cried. "Meat Hook and Bullet Head!"

The two mutant leaders had gone for the cigarette boat. Somehow they were able to climb into the long vessel. Everyone was surprised when the engines came to life in back of the boat. Kirkland had fixed them the second time.

Meat Hook pushed the throttle to the maximum. The boat roared away. Shots rang out from the native boats, but they all fell short. Meat Hook and Bullet Head were heading south, back to Lost Island.

"We can't let them get away!" Len cried. "They're almost out of sight!"

"Get them," Miles hollered. "They can't—"

Suddenly a ball of flame flashed on the horizon. The sound of the explosion rolled over the sea. The cigarette boat had gone up like a rocket. A billow of dark smoke punctuated the demise of Meat Hook and Bullet Head.

"The boat exploded!" Sir Charles cried.

"Vapor lock," Kirkland muttered. "Told you it would—ohh—"

A death rattle rose from Kirkland's chest. His head fell limply to one side. There was nothing they could do to bring him back. He had died from the mutant arrow.

Sir Charles stood on the beach, watching as the natives cleaned up the mess in the waters offshore.

Len and Miles sat with Colgan. Johnny Kahana also sat next to them with his arms around his daughter. They were all stunned, silent. Len and Miles couldn't believe their nightmare was really over. They had been on the beach for nearly two hours, waiting to head back to Papua.

"Hey, you guys were right! There is a compound up there!"

Andrew Stone ran over the beach. He had a camera in his hand. He had been taking pictures of the compound for his story.

"I found it," Stone said. "It was weird. I thought I saw something strange up there. It was this kid and these dogs."

Len stood up. "Augie!"

"We have to find him," Sir Charles said.

Miles also got to his feet. "No! Let Len and me go. You'll never find him. He may talk to us."

Len and Miles started toward the jungle. They entered the dense undergrowth, moving through the shadows. They had almost reached the base of the plateau when a dog moved out on the path in front of them. The animal sat down as if it wanted to prevent them from passing.

"Hi, guys."

Len and Miles wheeled to see Augie standing behind them. Augie held a gray puppy in his hands. He was smiling like a proud father.

"Look," he said. "One of the dogs had puppies. This is little Commando."

Len grimaced. "Augie—"

"No," Miles said. "Let me try. Augie, we're

134

going home. The mutants are dead. Mae's people came to take us back."

A frown spread over Augie's face. "No! I won't go. You can't make me."

"Please," Miles said. "You've got to—"

"I can't go," Augie told them. "I've got to stay here with little Commando. He needs me."

"This is crazy," Len said.

As soon as Len took a step toward Augie, the dog pack came out of the jungle. They circled around Augie, protecting him.

Augie smiled at Len and Miles. "It's okay, guys. I like it here. I'll be fine. See you!"

Augie disappeared into the jungle, carrying little Commando with him. They could hear him for a few minutes, but then the noise died. The jungle had swallowed Augie and the dog pack.

"I can't believe it," Len said.

Miles shook his head. "Someday, maybe we'll come back for him."

They moved down the path, following it back to the beach.

Sir Charles and Colgan wanted to go after Augie, but Miles convinced them that they would never find him. He told them to give Augie a few weeks and then send someone after him. He'd be ready to come back sooner or later.

Andrew Stone was busy writing it all down. "Kid stays with dog pack. Wild!"

A horn sounded offshore. The natives were waving at them. They had finished their task. It was time to leave the island.

They launched the small powerboat and climbed in. The boat joined the outriggers and other vessels. They started slowly to the west, making for Papua.

"Miles," Sir Charles said. "I've neglected to tell you how insistent your mother was to come with us."

Miles's eyes grew wide. "Really?"

Katherine hugged him. "I love you very much."

Sir Charles nodded. "Yes. And so do I."

A tear flowed down Miles's cheek. "Thanks, Dad."

They hugged each other.

The boats continued toward the west, away from Apocalypse Island. The boys had finally made it to freedom. And as they drifted in the vast ocean, neither Len nor Miles turned back for one last look at the landmass that grew smaller on the horizon.

Fourteen

The boys were gathered in a circle around Len and Miles. They had just finished soccer practice. Dover Academy had a big game the next day with Amesworth Academy, but the members of the team were more interested in the stories told by Len Hayden and Miles Bookman.

"Get out of here," one skeptic remarked. "You guys were lost on some deserted island with a bunch of killers."

Miles grinned. "I wouldn't lie to you."

"Right."

But some of the others were willing to believe a little. "Hey, what happened to that guy named Kirkland?"

"He was buried in his home town," Len replied.

"And that other kid stayed on the island with the dogs?"

Miles nodded. "They sent someone back but

they were never able to find Augie. They don't know if he's dead or alive."

"Aw, come on."

"Yeah, you guys are telling whoppers."

"I want to hear more about the native girl," someone said. "What happened to her?"

Miles reached into his pocket. "I got a letter from her yesterday. She's coming to visit us this summer."

Then he unfolded the latest issue of *World Explorer* magazine. He showed them the pictures of the compound and the bylines on the story. *Text by Andrew Stone and Sir Charles Bookman, as told by Len Hayden and Miles Bookman.*

"Cool!"

"They really did it!"

"That's not all," Miles said. "Check this out."

Miles unfolded a newspaper clipping. The boldfaced headline read, *Senator Williams Resigns over Secret Pacific Project.* The sub-heading said, *House of Horrors Revealed on Deserted Island.*

The boys carefully pored over the printed proof of their adventure. Len and Miles had deliberately waited until the publications were out before they told their story. They knew that no one would believe them without verification.

"So Meat Hook was real," one of the boys said.

Len shuddered. "Too real."

"What ever happened to that pilot guy you told us about?"

"He's cool," Len said. "Bookman's father fixed everything. Colgan is flying again. He has the best rescue record of any Coast Guard pilot."

"Wild."

"I wish I could've been there."

"No, you don't!" Len replied.

"It was horrible, guys," said Miles. "I still have nightmares."

"Me, too," Len said.

They continued to talk until the coach moved in to send them to the showers. Len and Miles lingered for a moment on the soccer field. Even though they had been through the adventure together, they still found it hard to believe, even with the stories in the newspapers and magazines.

"You really have dreams?" Len asked.

"Every night. I see Meat Hook's face."

"He's dead," Len replied.

"Who knows."

A cold wind blew over the soccer field. It was the end of October. Most of the leaves had already fallen from the trees around Portsmouth. It was going to be a cold, New Hampshire winter.

They started to walk toward the locker room.

"Mom says you can spend Thanksgiving with

139

us again this year," Len said. "It's cool with Dad, too."

Miles smiled and shook his head. "Sorry, Hayden. I can't make it this year. I've got other plans."

Len squinted at him. "What?"

"Mom and Dad are coming to see me," Miles replied.

"Get out of town! Both of them!"

Miles nodded. "We're going to spend Christmas together, too."

"You can still come over and have dinner with us," Len offered. "Your mom and dad will be welcome."

"Great," Miles replied. "I'll talk it over with Mom and Dad."

He threw his arm around Len's shoulders. Lost Island would always be with them. They would never put it completely behind them.

As the cold wind swept down, chilling them, it was good to be home.